When A Savage Falls For A Good Girl 3:

A Crazy Hood Love

Tina J

Copyright 2018

Zahra

"It's ok mama." I picked Sasha up off the ground and rocked her back and forth. I had her on the bed in the motel, and left her to make a bottle. I didn't think she'd roll off because she was asleep. She must've woken up and looked for me.

The first night I bounced with Sasha, I stayed at a hotel a few towns over and had no intentions of ever returning. Unfortunately, my bank account was depleted somehow. What am I saying, Kruz most likely had the shit emptied out to keep me from running away. Anyway, my funds were very low and the only place I could think of to stay was in a motel. The one in town was the cheapest around and I really had no choice.

I wasn't too upset about it because I bet Kruz had people looking for me outside of town. If they thought I left, it would make it easier for me to move around here because no one would be looking for me. The only thing I had to do is find someone to put the room in their name. I went through my phone and dialed the number of a guy I met a while ago.

4

His name was Teddy and I met him outside the club the same night Kruz supposedly first met Rhythm. I told him then, I was in a relationship but he was persistent in giving me his number. I never called and when I did, I wasn't sure he'd remember me. He didn't at first, but still decided to meet up with me. Once he saw me, he licked his lips and I knew his nasty ass would be down for whatever.

Funny how I've been in the same motel Rhythm worked at for the past two months and no one knew. I had Teddy get one of his boys to put it in his name and I've been here ever since. He's been giving me money to buy milk, diapers and other things I needed for Sasha, in return the two of us been fucking like rabbits. He was nowhere near as good as the Garcia brothers but it was decent enough to keep me satisfied.

If anyone is wondering if I knew Kommon and Kruz were brothers, absolutely. Shit, he had photos in his house and so did his parents. He wasn't around much, which made it easier for me to sleep with him.

The night in the bar, I didn't expect to run into him but being mad at Kruz, drunk, horny and curious as to what it would be like to experience two brothers, I took a chance. I had no idea the rendezvous would turn into a year of amazing sex between brothers. Of course, it was different but the thrill of it all, kept me doing it.

I could see how hurt Kruz was and if he let me move in, none of this would've happened. Kommon claimed I was the woman he wanted to marry but it had been three years before I met him and he hadn't even asked yet. Now he's with the Rhythm bitch, moved her in and now expecting. If he wanted the same with me, why did he take so long?

"Shit." I glanced at the knot forming on Sasha's head and became nervous. She's still a baby and any injury could be bad, especially; a head one. I called Teddy and asked if he could pick me up and take me to the hospital but he was outta town. I looked out the window to see if Rhythm's car was there and when I didn't see it, I rushed to call a cab and went straight to the ER.

"It's ok pretty girl." The doctor said when he came in. He asked what happened and I told him she was crawling and bumped her head on the table. If I told them she fell, I'd have to deal with social services and I'm not beat.

"We're going to do a cat scan to make sure nothing's wrong and keep her overnight for observation." The nurse put an IV in her arm and pushed some Tylenol through to alleviate pain. I made a call and waited for the person to arrive.

An hour went by and the doctor said everything was fine. She was placed on the pediatric floor and the room they had her in was quiet. There was another crib but no one occupied it. I sat it the chair and rested my head. Sasha had fallen asleep and I turned on the television. A few minutes later the door opened, closed and she stepped over to check on my daughter.

WHAP! She smacked fire from my ass and I jumped up.

"Why in the fuck did you disappear with my grandbaby?" She tossed her purse on the windowsill.

"He was gonna kill me and if he weren't, Jamaica is because of what happened to Kalila."

"You should've left Sasha."

"My daughter needs her mother."

"You sound stupid. How the hell are you gonna raise a child on the run?"

"As long as she's with me, she'll be fine. Kids grow up without their fathers all the time."

"Without mothers too. Do you know the position you put me in with Kruz?" I stood, grabbed my purse and asked her to sit there while I went out.

"Where are you going?" I asked for her keys and when she didn't give them to me, I snatched them out her hand.

"I have someplace to be." I stormed out and let the nurses know her grandmother is in the room with her.

****

"You have some nerve showing your face after the shit you pulled." Tania said when she opened the door.

"Move." I pushed past her and went to the mini bar she had for a drink.

"She deserved it."

"Kruz and Jamaica are still asking questions Zahra. I don't know why I did that shit for you?" She snatched the glass out my hand and stared in my face. She's the one who attempted to destroy Rhythm's credit for me.

See, Ramon is cool with Jamaica and Kruz because all of them went to school together. I think he graduated with Kommon but they're all acquainted. I met him a few times when I went to the bank with Kruz and he seemed like a down to earth person. Very nice and was about his business. Unbeknownst to him, I started asking questions to benefit myself. I asked when he worked and pretended to be interested in wanting a home loan.

I found out the information needed and told Tania, who I grew up with. She worked at the same bank but was doing mad crooked shit. When she told me all the stuff she could get away with, I paid her a hefty amount of money to fuck up Rhythm's credit. She didn't care because the money was good. She did that shit in minutes and even made it look like the transactions occurred in a different bank. To this day, they still don't know how it happened but they did put out a fraud case, which meant it didn't mess up anything. I was pissed when my mother told me that because the bitch didn't deserve anything.

She had a baby father with money who was actually in his life. Yet; she's running around with my baby daddy tryna wife him up. Doesn't the bitch know that I'm Zahra Bell and he ain't going nowhere? They better recognize this bitter ex or should I say they should've. I told them from the beginning how I'd be so I don't know why everyone acting all surprised.

"You did it because you're money hungry."

"Whatever. Why you here?" She had her arms folded across her chest like my presence was bothering her.

"Sasha fell off the bed and I had to rush her to the hospital."

"Bitch, why you here? You should be at the hospital with her."

"Because her grandmother is there."

"Kruz, is gonna have a fit." I rolled my eyes because she had no idea what was going on and I had no intentions on telling her. People may be aware we broke up but I still tell them we fucking and he stays at my house to save face. I'll be damned if I look like a fool for him.

"I'm about to go." She picked her stuff up and walked to the door. I poured another shot, drank, and left out with her.

"Zahra, they better not ever find out." Tania shouted at her car.

"They won't damn."

"Fuck you bitch. Don't bring your ass to my house anymore." I sat in the car and rested my head on the steering wheel. Those two shots had my head spinning that quick. I lifted my head and noticed a car ride by and followed it. If this is who I think it is, I wanna see where they're going.

RING! RING! The cell phone I took with the keys rang. I answered and instantly caught an attitude at what I saw in front of my eyes.

"WHAT?"

"Sasha won't stop crying."

"Give her a damn bottle." Why the hell she acting like she never took care of a damn baby?

"Zahra, she wants her mother."

11

"You're her grandmother. Do your fucking job and babysit."

"Who the hell you talking to?"

"You. Now don't call this phone again. I'll be there, when I get there."

"Zahra, come get this baby."

"Fuck that baby." I disconnected the call and continued following the car.

"Be careful babe." Rhythm kissed me on the way out the door.

"I will." I looked around the area and an eerie feeling washed over me. I'm not worried about Zahra tryna run up on her or Kalila because they can hold their own. This feeling felt more like someone else.

"Keep these doors locked and don't open them for anyone."

"I'm not."

"I mean it Rhythm." I hated leaving her at Ms. Bell's house but we were there when Jamaica called and mentioned Kandy's boyfriend was in the area. We had been looking for him too and this is the time to get his ass. But the feeling wasn't going away.

"Ok babe. Just hurry back." I kissed her, ran down the steps and hopped in my truck.

On the ride over, I noticed a car following me. Each turn I made, so did the person. I pulled over, waited for them to go by but they turned down a different street. If I had time to follow them I would. Whoever it is obviously didn't want me to see them and it's all good because if it's meant for us to run in to one another, we will.

I hit the block Jamaica was on, pulled up next to him and asked where he at. Unfortunately, dude bounced but Kandy was hiding in some hotel. Crazy part about this whole situation, is her father has been helping us find her. Evidently, he didn't care for her due to the shit she caused. If you asked me, I think it goes further than that. There's no way a man will be ok with anyone purposely tryna murder their child no matter how old they are.

"What's up with Geoffrey?"

"I can't even tell you. One minute he was at the place and the next, he's gone. It's obvious he has someone working with him again."

"Yea but who?" He ran his hand over his head.

"Hold on." He answered his phone and I could hear him yelling about something.

"Yo! We gotta go." Jamaica hopped in the car and had me rush to my parents' house.

"What's the rush?"

"Your pops called and said to get here quick. He's been tryna reach you but you ain't answering." I felt my phone vibrating a few times but I was worried about the feeling I had around Rhythm and with the person following me, I forgot to check it.

I jumped out when we pulled up and saw at least five cop cars. My father was sitting on the couch with Kash and a police officer. Others were standing around listening t the cop ask questions.

"What's wrong? Why the cops here?" I looked straight at Kash.

"Nigga, you better not had stole shit from nobody." He looked up with tears in his eyes. If he crying that ain't the reason because he don't cry for shit.

"Tha fuck is going on?"

"Kruz, they found your mother's car abandoned on the side of the road."

"Ok."

"It was set on fire and they think your mother was in it." I fell against the wall and leaned my head on it. My mother and I weren't seeing eye to eye but death isn't something I wished on her. Is this the feeling I had?

"Hello." I heard my father answer the house phone as a detective and more cops entered.

"Are you sure?" Everyone stopped speaking and waited for him to hang up.

"Get to the hospital Kruz."

"Why?" I instantly thought Rhythm or Axel was hurt and headed to the door.

"A baby was brought in with a head injury and they think it might be Sasha."

"Say what? I know you didn't just say a head injury."

"Hurry up son because if it is her this may be your chance to get her." He gave me a look that really meant for me to get Zahra.

The detective that walked in started telling me it's the reason he came over. The doctor called social services and reported the injury. They ran Sasha's information in the system and found out I'm her father, which brought them here.

"Call me as soon as you hear something about ma."

"I will."

"Kash you good?" He had tears falling down his face and I could tell he was hurting. He ran over and hugged me.

"You think mommy ok?"

"She's gonna be fine. You know she's to mean for anything to happen to her."

"Go get my niece and you know what to do with her mother." He wiped his eyes and backed away. I ran out the house with Jamaica on my heels.

I sped in and outta traffic tryna get to the hospital. It didn't matter how much I went over the speed limit or if I cop would pull me over. If my daughter was here, I had to get there before Zahra bounced with her again and I couldn't find her. We ran in the hospital and straight into Kommon.

"Tha fuck you doing here?" His girl turned around and that's when I realized she's the same chick who came to see Kalila in that tight ass outfit.

17

"I've been calling you." I couldn't say anything because I put his ass on block the minute I got bailed outta jail so it's possible.

"What you want?"

"Zahra called talking about I needed to get to the hospital because something happened to my niece."

"FUCK!" I ran over to the nurse's desk and asked what room Sasha was in. She told me and all of us ran to the elevator. If she had a room number it meant she's still here.

I felt my brother staring at me and could tell he wanted to say something. Thankfully, the elevator doors opened beforehand. I stepped off and noticed security at the door of a room and prayed it wasn't Sasha's. Unfortunately, I wasn't lucky so when the nurse pointed to the door, my heart dropped. The closer I got, the faster it started to beat.

"I can't go in." Security asked who we were and just as I went to step in, I felt someone fall into me.

"Oh my God, Kommon." Sabrina dropped to her knees as his body slid down. Blood was pouring outta his stomach.

"Oh shit." Jamaica yelled and pulled his gun out.

18

"Motherfucker did you just shoot my brother?"

"It's supposed to be you but y'all look so much alike, I fucked up. But this one won't miss." I smirked as Jamaica pulled back the trigger.

BOOM! BOOM! TATTTT! TATTTTT! Shots rang out and people were running everywhere.

"Where the hell are the shots coming from?" I pulled my brothers body inside the room they said Sasha was in, made sure Jamaica was good and closed the door.

"I couldn't see but I'm hit." Jamaica pulled his pant leg up and he had two bullets in his calf.

"How's Kommon?" I asked Sabrina who had her hands on his stomach tryna stop the bleeding.

"He's losing a lot of blood." I took my shirt off and put it on his wound. Jamaica was already using his belt to tie up his leg.

"Who the hell is shooting out there?" I turned around and couldn't believe my eyes. What the fuck is going on?

"Hey handsome." I kissed lil Kenron on his cheek. Jamaica and Kruz ran out so fast he didn't get a chance to drop her off at home and Kruz told me to stay here. It's not a problem because we're always here anyway.

"Mommy can I hold him?" Axel sat next to me and put his arms out. He loved Kenron Jr. and couldn't wait for me to have my baby.

"Daddy's having another baby too with Caroline."

"He is?"

"Yup."

"Wow. You're going to be a big brother to two babies and a big cousin to lil Kenron."

"I know and I'm gonna tell them what to do like a boss."

"What?"

"Kash bosses me around mommy. He says, because he's the oldest I have to do what he tells me." My radar went up quick because I'm whooping Kash ass myself if he got Axel stealing.

"What does he tell you to do?" I kept my hand under Kenron's head for support.

"He makes me get him snacks and juices out the kitchen. He said daddy Kruz doesn't let him eat at our house." I busted out laughing. I did like how close they became because Axel doesn't have any friends. He's always at one of his grandparents or at his fathers.

Kruz was definitely strict with Kash in the house and I thought about discussing it with him but I understand why he's that way. Besides him and his father, Kash pretty much got away with a lotta stuff.

The day Axel asked if he could call him daddy Kruz, I sat him down and told him to speak with his father. It's not like I had to ask but Axel's father is involved in his son's life and I wanted to make sure he's ok with it. Granted, my son can do it if he wants but both Kruz and I thought out of respect, the least he can do is let his father know.

Shockingly, his father didn't mind. Him and Kruz have yet to speak face to face but they've spoken on the phone plenty of times and exchanged phone numbers. I really had good people in my life and I thank God everyday for them.

"Daddy Kruz gives him a hard time but he loves him."

"I know. Mommy, he spit up. Yuk." He tried to push him off his lap.

"Axel you spit up on me all the time as a baby. My son can't do the same to you?" Kalila came down after taking a bath. It's the first one since she gave birth and I swear she was in there for almost an hour.

"No TiTi. I'm a kid." She ran after and tickled him until he had tears coming down his face.

I changed Kenron and asked her to grab a bottle. Axel went in the kitchen to eat a snack while Kalila and I sat in the living room watching the news.

"We're live at the scene where a gunman or men have opened fire on the pediatric floor of this hospital behind me. Officers are telling us they're not sure if it's a hostage situation but they've been told they're some fatalities." I turned the channel just as Axel came in and started playing with his

LEGO's on the floor. I hated those things. Anyone who has kids knows how bad it hurts to step on them.

"Who in the hell would shoot up a hospital and the pediatric floor at that?" She spoke low and I shook my head. It's very unfortunate that people will risk their life doing dumb shit.

DING DONG! The doorbell rang and we looked at each other. Axel had his earphones in thank God because he would've asked who it was.

I put Kenron in the swing and walked over to peek with Kalila. We may have learned our lesson at the hotel but we still nosy. The person had a baseball cap on with a coat and you couldn't see their face.

DING DONG! It rang again and the person turned around. It was Stacy from across the street.

"You think we should open it?"

"No." Kalila said and I agreed. We both went to sit and outta nowhere the front door opened.

"How you two heffas sitting here and didn't open the door?" Stacy bitched walking in with Kalila's mom.

23

"We just came downstairs. What's up?" She peeked out the window and all of us looked at her.

"CLOSE THE DOOR!" She yelled at Kalila, who was standing there about to do just that.

"Why are you yelling?" She hurried to shut it and I picked my phone up to text Kruz. Something ain't right if she's here and screaming for us to close the door.

"Y'all need to get outta here." I grabbed Axel and Kalila snatched Kenron up gently.

"What's going on?"

"Word on the street is your sister hired some guy to shoot this house up." Ms. Bell covered her mouth.

"But how? No one has heard from her."

"I don't know but it's supposed to happen tonight."

"All of a sudden, you heard loud music and then cars screeching outside.

"RUNNNNN!!!!!" Stacey yelled and all of us ran in the basement. There's a door down there that leads outside.

BOOM! You could hear what sounded like the door being kicked in. Axel started crying and asking for his father or daddy Kruz.

"THEY'RE IN THE BASEMENT. HURRY UP AND GET THEM."

"Oh my God. Run Kalila and Rhythm. Don't look back."

"Ma, let's go." Her and Stacy stayed back and told us not to stop running with the kids.

POW! POW! POW! POW! You heard gunshots and both of us stopped to turn around.

"I have to go back."

"Kalila we can't. We'll send the guys." Both of us had tears coming down our face as we tried ducking behind cars. We knocked on a few doors and no one answered.

A car flew past us and did a spin at the end of the street. When we saw it coming back in our direction we dipped behind a van. I covered Axel's mouth and Kalila rocked Kenron to keep him from crying.

"They out here because I just saw them." My heart was beating fast, pains were developing in my stomach as the voices and footsteps got closer.

"Take Axel and run the other way. I'll be a distraction." I told Kalila who's eyes were big as hell.

"Sounds like a plan to me." The man's voice said over my head. Once again, I'm saying a prayer to God hoping he spares my son and Kenron Jr.

"Take Axel and run the other way. I'll be a distraction." *I told Kalila whose eyes were big as hell.*

"Sounds like a plan to me." The man's voice said over my head. Once again, I'm saying a prayer to God hoping he spares my son and Kenron Jr.

"What are you doing here?" I asked Drew when my eyes finally opened. He reached out for me and another guy helped Kalila with Kenron.

"Some shit went down at the hospital and Kruz said you needed help." I wiped my eyes and looked in the sky thanking God for saving us again.

"But how did you know?" He gave me a *duh* look but I still wanted to know the answer.

"We can discuss that later. Let's go." All of us hopped in the dark Tahoe and waited for the guy driving to pull off.

"Is my mother ok?" Kalila asked with tears falling down her face.

"Which lady was your mom?" He was texting on his phone. The other guy sped off and told us to get as low as possible.

"SHIT!"

TATTTTTTT! TATTTTTTTTT! I covered Axel's ears and used my body to shield him and Kalila did the same with Kenron. I felt a pain in my leg and stayed put. If I got up its no telling if Axel would be hit. After a few minutes the guys told us we could sit up.

"What's that mommy?" He pointed to the red liquid coming down my leg. Kalila looked at me and Drew did the same.

"We gotta get you to a hospital."

"Which one because the other one is locked down." The other guy said.

"FUCK! Kruz is gonna be pissed."

"I'm fine. Can y'all take my son to his father please?" I felt Kalila grabbing my hand and Axel was on my lap with his head on my shoulder.

"You need a doctor." I refused to see how bad the wound was until my son was safe. I was too scared I'd panic and scare him.

"Please take him to his father and then we can go to the hospital." Both guys looked at each other and then me.

"What's his address?" I gave it to him and ten minutes later we were in front of the house. I text Axel on the way because I still had my phone on me. When we got there, he was standing at the door waiting.

My son jumped out and ran straight to him. I could see his body shaking and felt like shit for not protecting him better. He put him down and told him to go inside.

"Are you ok?" Axel had concern written on his face and regardless of the pain I was in, I told him yes. He ran his hand down my cheek and I thought Drew would kill him when he put the gun to the back of his head.

"You know damn well she's married and he don't play another nigga touching her." Axel put his hands up and backed away.

"Drew please take the gun off him."

"Rhythm, you know…"

"I do know but he is my sons' father and I don't need him looking out the window and seeing you holding a gun on him."

"Fine! But Kruz will know about this." He put it away and lit a cigarette.

"Rhythm, this isn't ok. You have my son around them and you were shot. I'm gonna request full custody of him because it's clear you can't keep him safe." He moved from the car and even with my leg feeling like it would fall off, I walked behind him fast as hell.

"Kruz had nothing to do with this Axel. This is happening because of the bitch you fucked." He turned to me.

"What bitch?"

"Zahra." I folded my arms.

"Yea, you thought I didn't know about the fling y'all had years ago. She did this Axel because I'm the bitch she hates. The bitch who got the good men, while she had to do whatever to keep one."

"Rhythm, that was years ago."

"Exactly but the hatred a person carries for you never goes away."

"I doubt she did anything involving guns." I chuckled at his ignorance. Axel is not a street dude so he really doesn't know the ins and outs of the streets, except for what he hears or watches on television.

"You know she told our son she hated me and if she could kill me, she would?"

"WHAT?"

"So think again if you believe she's not capable of this." I pointed to my leg and the truck riddled with bullet holes. It's a miracle I'm the only one who got hit.

"I haven't brought him around her since she said it before you asked." Axel stood there quiet.

"He's scared of what she said and honestly, I'm in shock she pulled this off myself but you of all people know, I would never intentionally place my son in danger. Axel look." I felt a dizziness rush over me and held on to the wall of his house.

"You know I had no idea this would happen and if I thought for one minute he was in harm's way, I'd bring him to you. Please don't take my son from me." I felt the tears running down my face as the pain became worse and the thought of him taking my son hit me full force.

"You need a doctor."

"FUCK A DOCTOR. DON'T TAKE MY SON AXEL!" I shouted and felt my body falling.

"Mommy!" Is all I hear and passed out before I hit the ground.

****

"Thank God you're awake." Caroline said and walked over with my mother. I was surprised to see her because we're not close at all.

"Where's my son? Caroline please don't let him take my son from me." I tried to sit up and the machines were going berserk. I snatched as many monitors I could off and attempted to get out the bed. There was a bandage and huge brace on my leg preventing me from doing so.

"Honey, what are you talking about?" My mom was about to cry herself.

"Please. I can't live without my son. Mommy, don't let him take Axel."

"Calm down Rhythm. No one is taking Axel away from you." Caroline said and smiled.

"Axel said he's taken my son away from me because of what happened. I swear, I'll kill him myself if he takes him."

"What's going on and why is she so upset?" The doctor came rushing in with two nurses.

"I have to get outta here." I lifted my hand on my head and there was a bandage there too. I must've hit the ground hard.

"Mrs. Garcia, you suffered a head injury and needed a few stitches. Your baby is going to go in distress if you don't calm down." My hands then went to my stomach and I remembered my child. I watched as the nurse inserted a liquid in my IV.

"What the fuck is that?"

33

"Mrs. Garcia, it's a small dose of Ativan to keep you calm." She smiled and leaned down to my ear.

"Kruz said he'd kill me if I let anything happen to you and the baby so please relax." She whispered and backed away.

"Where is my husband?"

"He'll be here soon." I peeked around my mom and noticed his father and Kash walking in.

"Caroline, I know we had words here and there in the beginning but please don't let him take my son."

"He's not Rhythm and I cursed his ass out for even entertaining some shit like that." She came closer.

"We all know how much you love your son and would never let anything happen to him. I think he's scared too but I promise you, if he even thinks about trying to do it behind my back, I'll kill him for you." I grabbed her hand and thanked her for having my back.

She and I had some choice words in the start of their relationship but we've been cordial since. I know how much she loves my son too and I'm thankful she didn't leave Axel after all the stuff he put her through.

"Wait! Where's Kalila?" They all gave me a look.

"Where is she?" I asked one more time before the medication put me to sleep.

After I drug my brother in the room and checked on Jamaica, my phone started going off nonstop. I took it off the clip and saw the message Rhythm sent. I knew then, my eerie feeling was right. I hurried and sent a message to Drew telling him to get there fast.

I removed my shirt and pushed down on Kommon's wound. Blood was pouring out like crazy but nothing could prepare me for who I saw.

"How the fuck are you here?" I asked my mother who looked terrified at the blood leaving my brothers body.

"What do you mean? What happened to Kommon?" She put Sasha in the crib and fell to her knees. I took my gun out, opened the door and went to find some doctors.

The floor was quiet and there were people laid out groaning and asking for help. I walked past the bodies with my gun still drawn, and came across some dude dressed in black barely clinging to life. I wanted to question him but it had to wait because both of my brothers needed help.

I went behind the nurses' desk and saw a few of them with their knees up, holding hands. I reached out for one and asked her to page some doctors and let the police know the floor was clear as of now. I could see how terrified they were but it's not the time to piss me off.

A few minutes later cops came rushing through the doors with doctors and tech's behind them. I stood there and gestured for them to go in Sasha's room and shortly after they came out with Kommon, and another tech came out with Jamaica who looked pale as hell. Sabrina was hysterical crying and so was my mother.

I helped Sabrina up and told her to go in the bathroom to clean herself off. When she came out, I asked if she could take Sasha home with her. She didn't wanna leave Kommon but I reminded her there's nothing she can do right now but wait.

I told her as soon as I hear something, I'd call or send someone to pick her up from Kommon's house. I hated to ask her to leave her man but I couldn't leave Sasha here and I damn sure ain't sending her with my mother.

"What the fuck are you doing here?" I gripped my mother's arm, pushed her in the room and closed the door. I didn't care about the blood on the floor, nor did I care about her crying.

"Zahra called and told me Sasha was here. I came up to see if she were ok, Zahra ran out and took my car and cell phone. I tried calling you from the hospital phone but no one answered." I glanced down at my phone and noticed missed calls.

I didn't pay it any mind because Rhythm needed help. I pressed play on the voicemail and put it on speaker. I wanted to hear what her message was.

"Kruz, this is your mother. I'm at the hospital with Sasha. Zahra said she hit her head but I don't think it's the truth because the knot is too big. The doctor called social services and they may try and take her. Get up here fast." I hung the phone up and started clapping my hands. My mother looked confused.

"You put on one hell of a show mother."

"What are you talking about Kruz? I called you."

38

"That you did, but my question is why didn't you call, when she called you? Huh?" I stepped in her face.

"I COULD'VE HAD THAT BITCH IF YOU CALLED WHEN SHE TOLD YOU TO COME UP HERE. WHY ARE YOU SAVING HER? WHAT THE FUCK IS REALLY GOING ON BECAUSE YOU CAN'T BE GOING THIS HARD FOR A BITCH WHO KIDNAPPED YOUR GRANDDAUGHTER, SET YOUR CAR ON FIRE TO MAKE US THINK YOU WERE DEAD AND SHOT YOUR OTHER SON THINKING IT WAS ME." I didn't care how loud I was. She was hysterical crying and all I could do is stare out the window to keep from choking her.

"What up Drew? Did you get there in time?" I asked when I picked up. Rhythm was on my mind but with so much going on, I couldn't get to her.

"Say what?" He started telling me how my wife was shot, her ex ran his hand down her face, threatened to take Axel and she passed out and hit the ground.

"I'll handle it when I get outta here. Do me a favor and send a few guys there to watch over her. I want you back at Ms.

Bell's house with Trevor to find out what the fuck went down and who it was." We said our goodbyes and I turned back to my mother.

"You out here protecting Zahra and she hired someone to shoot up my wife's, best friend's house." My mother covered her mouth.

"WITH THEM IN IT!"

"Oh my God."

"AND THE KIDS WERE THERE." I tried my hardest not to put my hands on her but each second passing made it harder for me.

"SHE THREATENED TO TELL YOUR FATHER I WAS GETTING HIGH."

"Tha fuck you just say?" I couldn't have been hearing my mother right. She doesn't get high.

"SHE CAUGHT ME IN THE ALLEY GIVING A GUY ORAL SEX FOR DRUGS!" I could see the embarrassment and petrified look on her face.

"You got to be fucking kidding me."

"It's the truth Kruz."

"I would hope you ain't making some nasty shit like this up."

"I'm not. Kruz, your father was cheating on me with the lady from the post office and I found out."

"WHAT?" I had no idea they were going through anything because my pops sure acts like it's all about my mom.

"I couldn't take it and became depressed."

"Depressed?"

"Yes, depressed. I made a doctor's appointment and he gave me some pills to help. Unfortunately, the high wasn't staying long enough to keep me from my reality." I could tell she was hurt by speaking on it.

"Each day he walked in the house I didn't know if he came from being with her or not and I didn't want to deal with it." She walked over to the window and continued talking.

"The pain was too bad Kruz and I had to get higher to alleviate the hurt." I stood there in shock.

"I'm sorry son. I'm so fucking sorry for hurting you and not having your back but I couldn't let her tell your father.

I didn't want my kids to be ashamed of me." She put her head down.

"HOLD THE FUCK UP!" I had to rub my temples.

"Pops is cheating on you?" She nodded her head.

"Does he know, you know? Wait! How long has this been going on?" I'm still at a loss for words finding out my pops was a cheater, especially; when he instilled being loyal to our women growing up.

"I filed for divorce but he won't let me leave him."

"When?"

"A year and a half ago."

"What? How the fuck did Zahra catch you?"

"It was on a Saturday night and your father claimed to be at your uncle Shawn's house playing cards. I didn't believe him because him and Shawn aren't that close. I hopped in my car and rode to your uncle's house and his car wasn't there. I called his phone and he answered telling me he was there. Instead of mentioning I knew he was lying, I went from hotel to hotel looking for him and at the last one, there was his car."

"But how you know he wasn't there for a meeting" I was thinking of anything to give my pops the benefit of the doubt.

"Kruz, I sat outside the place for five hours and when he finally emerged, it was hand in hand with the woman from the post office."

"Are you sure?"

"Positive. I know who she is because she delivers our mail and she can't be any older than thirty maybe thirty-five."

"Damn." My pops was someone's sugar daddy.

"I know. Anyway, they went to the car and engaged in a kiss that he should've only given me. I jumped out the car, walked up and beat the daylights outta her. It wasn't until your father screamed out she was pregnant did I stop."

"What?" My mother had snot and tears all over her face.

"I was devastated that not only did he cheat but got her pregnant. I sped off and stayed away for two days but not without your father calling my phone threatening me."

"Why was he threatening you when you caught him?'
She shrugged her shoulders.

"When I came home, he showed me a paper saying the woman terminated the pregnancy and that it was over. I still couldn't deal and fell into a deeper depression. Long story short, I went out to see if drugs would help ease the pain and ran into some guy who had just passed some drugs off to a white woman. I walked up and asked what he had, went to get money out and realized I left my purse home. I asked if he could give me credit and I'd be back to pay him and he said no. I had to find another way of payment."

"So you suck him off?" I was mad as hell hearing her story.

"I needed to escape the pain Kruz and it may not be what you wanted to hear but its why I went hard for her. I was ashamed and didn't want it to come out."

"I don't even know what to say."

"I didn't know anything about Zahra and Kommon but you were right. I should've told you about them knowing one another. I'm sorry Kruz." She slid down the wall crying. I had no words and walked out the room. I mean what can I say to that? My mother was hurting, so she resulted in acting like a fiend and my ex caught her.

My mind was gone at the moment, yet; I had no time to dwell on it or vent because my wife and two brothers are laid up in hospital beds. Zahra somehow escaped and we don't know who shot up Ms. Bell's house. What else could go wrong?

"CODE BLUE IN THE OPERATING ROOM! CODE BLUE IN THE OPERATING ROOM!" Why in the hell did I even ask?

****

It's been five hours and I'm still sitting in the same hospital waiting on my brother Kommon to come outta surgery. The code blue was on him because he flatlined twice. It tore me up inside because I was supposed to hear his story weeks ago about the shit with Zahra and hadn't made it to his house. I wanted to but things got in the way and I kept pushing it back.

My mother is still here but sitting on the other side of the room. I was fucked up in the head about what she told me

45

too. I understand her being weak for a man she's been married to all those years but to result in drugs is something I can't get past.

Then, to get caught giving a guy head outside the place in return for them is killing me the most. I don't even care if people found out because drug addicts run in every family whether they admit or not. My beef with her is going hard for Zahra and not coming clean sooner. At least, most of this BS could've been avoided. My ex would've been dead, my wife wouldn't be in the hospital and we could focus strictly on this shit with Jamaica's ex.

"Garcia Family." Me and my mother stood. The doctor walked us in a room and closed the door.

"Hold up!" We heard as he shut the door. It was my father and Kash.

"Is my son ok?"

"I was just getting ready to discuss it with them." All of us took a seat and I wanted to address the shit with my father but decided to wait because it's not the time.

"Mr. Garcia suffered a gunshot wound to the abdomen. We almost lost him twice due to the massive amount of blood loss, and because his sugars were very high we had to give him insulin as well. We had to cut out some of his intestines because they were severely damaged. He has to keep the colostomy bag on until he can use the bathroom on his own."

"Sugars were high?" Kommon had diabetes since we were little and the only time his sugars were off is if he were stressing and going through some shit. He'd forget to take his insulin and my parents would dig in his ass.

"Extremely high." He finished telling us how he'll be in ICU for a week and that he needs 24/7 care for at least six weeks. I didn't worry about that because Sabrina would be right there and if he needed a nurse, I'd pay for one. We shook his hand and thanked him for making sure my brother made it.

"I'll be back."

"Where are you going?" Kash asked.

"To see my wife." I jetted out before anyone else could ask me a question or keep me longer than needed.

I called Kalila's phone and told her to let Sabrina know Kommon is outta surgery and I'll be by after seeing Rhythm to get Sasha, so she can go up there. I also told her to let Jamaica know people are outside his door and I'll be back. He came outta surgery two hours ago and was still asleep when I went to see him.

****

"I'm here for Rhythm Garcia." I told the nurse at the front desk of this hospital. The other one was still shut down and it was a bitch tryna get out but I left anyway. The lady told me where to go and that visiting hours would be over soon. Who the fuck cares? I'm still gonna be here.

I stepped in her room and smiled as she slept peacefully. Her mom and some other chick were sitting in a chair talking. The nurse Shayla, I had watching over her was someone we used for minor accident. When I found out which hospital she was at, I was happy because I knew someone there and if anything happened she'd call.

"Kruz." Her mom gave me a hug and told me what went down in so many words. She introduced me to the chick Caroline and it didn't take long for Axel to come in.

"We need to talk." I gestured with my eyes for him to turn around. This punk kept his son with him and he should've because I was gonna knock is fucking head off.

"Fine! I can say it right here." He had a smug look on his face.

"I'm not gonna talk long but just know if you choose to move forward with tryna take my stepson from his mother, that woman in there won't make it another day." He went to say something and I walked back in the room. I wasn't about to play no fucking games with him.

"Don't threaten me in front of my son." He had the nerve to say with Axel lying on his shoulder.

"What you talking about?" I sat on the bed next to Rhythm.

"You just said if I take my son from her, my wife would come up missing." I smirked because his punk ass in here acting like a bitch.

49

"Man, go head with that whining."

"I don't want you anywhere near my son." He tried to say it with his chest poked out. I stood and turned around.

"I'm tryna remain calm because my stepson is in your arms but don't tempt me." Rhythm was still asleep and I was trying my hardest not to lay him the fuck out.

"You don't scare me."

"Then put Axel down and let's discuss this outside like grown men." He looked at Rhythm's mom, his wife, son, and then me.

"Not right now. My son needs me." He gripped him tighter and I chuckled.

"Punks jump up to get beat down."

"Excuse me!"

"You heard me. Punks like you always jumping like you tough and then BAM!" I shouted.

"They get beat the fuck down." I whispered so lil Axel wouldn't hear me. I looked him up and down and smirked. I'm gonna have fun with this nigga.

"Hey baby." I reached out for Kruz who was sitting right there.

"You good?" I nodded my head yes and glanced around the room. My mother had Axel asleep on her lap and she had her head back on the windowsill dosing off.

"Kruz, he's tryna take Axel away from me." I whispered with tears falling down my face.

"Rhythm, you know I'd never allow that to happen."

"I know but.-"

"But nothing. Axel and I have an understanding so don't concern yourself with it. I promise, I got you." I nodded and asked him to carry me in the bathroom.

"Tell me what happened." I used the bathroom and brushed my teeth before talking. Husband or not, I smelled my own breath and it was horrible.

He found a washcloth, put soap on it and had me stand she could wash me up. Kruz was perfect in my eyes and I can't imagine him not being in my life.

"We were watching television and someone knocked at the door. We looked out the window but didn't answer." He shook his head laughing and said we were too damn nosy.

"Ms. Bell came in with Stacey, cursing us out behind her. She told us Zahra hired someone to shoot the house up. Baby, two minutes hadn't even gone by when she yelled out for us to run."

"Run where?"

"We ran in the basement and out the door. We heard shooting and..." I covered my mouth.

"Oh my God, is Ms. Bell ok?"

"She's good. Her and Stacey were able to get away and the dudes I sent with Drew must've scared the other guys off."

"Why did I here gunshots?"

"Because someone did get out the car and run up on the house. Drew said they got there just in time." I wrapped my arms around him as he continued washing me up.

"How did you get shot?"

"Someone started shooting at the truck. I used my body to shield Axel and the bullet must've come through the door. I

52

felt it but my concern was on Axel. Babe, I was so scared and then I got to his father's and he started threatening me with taking him. I didn't take the time out to realize how bad it was."

"It's all good and why that nigga have his hand in your face?" I rolled my eyes.

"Drew is a got damn snitch." He laughed.

"He's supposed to be. And you know Kalila, and now Sabrina would tell you."

"Whatever." He grabbed the towel and dried me off.

"Thanks for saving me."

"I wasn't there."

"You sent your people. If they hadn't come, we may not be here." I rubbed my stomach.

"I keep telling you, I got you Rhythm even if I'm not around." He helped me slide in some shorts my mom brought and put the shirt on.

"You're so good to me Kruz." I stared in his eyes and saw every bit of love he had for me in them.

"I'm supposed to be good to my wife." He and I engaged in a tender and passionate kiss. His hands my roamed my body and I couldn't help but get turned on.

"If you're mother wasn't here, I swear, I'd fuck the shit outta you in that hospital bed."

"Don't you worry baby. I definitely got some surprises for you." He carried me back it the room and Axel was waking up. I asked Kruz to lay him in the bed with me. At the age of seven, he's still a momma's boy.

"Mommy, why did daddy say he was taking me away?" I looked up at Kruz who now had his face turned up.

"He just meant for a few days. You see mommy's leg is hurt." I pointed to it.

"Daddy Kruz told him no and they should go outside to talk about it." He shrugged and I tried containing my laughter. I knew damn well Axel wasn't fucking with Kruz on any level.

"Daddy Kruz wanted to make sure I saw you when I woke up." He smiled and snuggled under me.

"Should I wake her?" He spoke about my mom who was knocked out.

"No, she's good. Come sit with me." He pulled the other chair up and sat next to me.

"I have to tell you what my mother told me." His head was resting on the side of me.

"Is it bad?"

"Yes and no. I'll talk to you about it later. I just need a little sleep."

"Go head baby." I rubbed his hair and a few minutes later he too, was asleep. I stared around at my family and smiled.

Me and my mother recently became close and she's been around ever since. My son is next to me with my husband, and the baby in my belly is fine, which reminds me. I pressed the button for the nurse to come put the monitors back on. I removed them to go in the bathroom. After she did, I dosed off with everyone else.

****

"Rhythm, you can't have him threatening me around my son." Axel walked in the hospital room with Caroline.

Kruz took Axel with him to change clothes, out to eat and check on Jamaica. I called Axel and asked him to come here. Now that I'm not dying, we needed to have a grown-up talk because throwing a tantrum is for kids.

"Axel, calm down." Caroline gave him a look and he seemed to be doing what she asked.

"I understand why you're mad but how did you think my husband would react after hearing you were tryna take my son from me?"

"He's our son Rhythm and if you can't keep him safe, then yes, it is my job to take him."

"I get it Axel but this wasn't his fault and neither of us can control if someone will attack us; not even you." He waved me off.

"I'm just saying Axel, you can walk out this hospital with our son and get hit by a stray bullet, hit by a car or whatever else."

"Not likely." He gave me a fake smile.

"Stop being a dick Axel. My son has never been in harm's way and you know it." He put his head down.

"I get you were scared; shit, I was too but I made sure to protect him. Hell, it's the reason I was shot and he wasn't."

"Rhythm, I want what's best for Axel and maybe he should stay with me until you can figure out who is trying to kill you." I lifted the covers off my leg and tried to stand.

"Nigga, it's the bitch you used to fuck with, whether it was over you or not, she's the one responsible. I told you that at the house."

"Zahra doesn't have it in her to do this."

"I guess you know her well enough, huh?" Caroline butted in and folded her arms.

"It was a long time ago Caroline."

"So what? It's obvious she hates Rhythm if she's doing this."

"You're not taking my son."

"I second that. Axel, we have more than enough room for him, but his home is with Rhythm and you know it."

"I'm his father." He stood.

"Exactly! How would your son feel knowing you're about to rip him from his mother? The one he's lived with all his life."

"He's a kid. He'll get over it."

"I'm warning you not to do this Axel." I said it in a stern voice.

"Are you threatening me too?"

"All I'm saying is, my son loves you and I would hate for him to lose you because of pettiness." I held my hands up and scooted back in the bed. He looked at Caroline.

"We all know who her husband is Axel and if he threatened you already and said, I'm gonna come up missing why would you risk it? Do you not love me? Am I not worthy enough to stay in your life?" I could see how upset she was getting and I don't blame her. If someone threatened my life, the last thing Kruz would do is put me in jeopardy.

"Caroline, I would never put you in harm's way."

"Then stop this madness about taking Axel." She grabbed his chin and made him look at her.

58

"Kruz loves Rhythm and Axel, and I can bet he's doing everything in his power to get the people who did this to her. Don't let your pride get you or me killed."

"I'm just saying Caroline."

"All I wanna hear you say is you'll stop this because if he comes looking for me, I'm telling him exactly where you are." I busted out laughing.

"Are you serious?"

"Yup because my babies need their mother and I'm not about to lose my life for you, even though you're playing with mine." She made him look at her.

"Axel, if its ever a choice of you or the kids; the kids will always win. It doesn't mean I love you any less, but my kids are gonna grow up and live happy lives." She started tearing up and he pulled her in for a hug.

"I'm sorry babe. You know I don't like seeing you upset."

"Then tell her it's over and I promise to do some extra nasty stuff to you later." I sucked my teeth because no one wanted to hear that.

"I want it real nasty too. I'm talking about in the…"

She shushed him with her finger.

"Whatever you want baby." They kissed and in walked my husband and son.

"DADDY!" Axel ran to him and Kruz turned his nose up.

"It's fine babe. He's not gonna do it."

"He better not or I was about to drop his ass in here and tell Axel he had a heart attack." He whispered in my ear and I tried not to laugh.

"Is it ok if he comes home with me?"

"Mommy doesn't care if I come with you, right mommy?"

"Right. Call me before you go to bed and thanks Caroline." She winked and grabbed Axel's hand on the way out.

"What changed his mind?" He had me scoot over and got in bed with me.

"You and his wife." I explained what went down and he laughed too.

"You better not ever throw me under the bus if a nigga says that shit."

"Never. I'm riding all the way baby." We kissed and his hand went under the covers. Let's just say we took care of each other and took a nap. I'm glad Axel got it together because I can see Kruz hurting him and I don't want that on my conscience, even if it is his own fault.

"How you feeling?" I opened my eyes to see Sabrina standing next to the bed.

"In pain. Did my brother get hit?"

"I'm good." I turned my head and Kruz was sitting in a chair with the woman I'm assuming is his wife.

"Hi." She walked over to me and put her hand out.

"I'm Rhythm, your sister in law and we're gonna give you two a few minutes." She took Sabrina's hand and left the room. Neither of us said a word at first.

"How did you end up with Zahra?" He came closer to the bed and leaned on the wall.

"A little over a year ago, I went to the bar for drinks. She was there flirting with me. I took her home, slept with her and we had been together ever since."

"Did she mention having a man?" I blew my breath and pushed the button to raise the bed a little.

"She did."

"And you stayed?"

"Yea because it was always, *I'm leaving him and give me a little time.* Sad to say, my feelings were involved and I believed her."

"So, you were like a nigga who claimed to leave his wife for the mistress?"

"You can say that. However; I left her alone for a few months, blocked her and told her not to contact me. Unfortunately, we ran into one another again and picked up where we left off."

"When did you find out I was her man?

"A few months before she delivered."

"Word?" he couldn't believe Zahra never told him and shit, I felt the same.

"I walked into ma and pops house to say hi because I was home for a few days. She was at the table and I had no idea why or how she found out who my parents were. It wasn't until ma shouted out she was your woman. Ma, stepped out the kitchen and I almost strangled her." He shook his head in disbelief.

"The last time I saw her at the house, she was complaining about you leaving her alone and some other shit I ain't wanna hear. She started talking about us being together again when no one was around. I told her let's go eat, had her meet me at a park, told her ass off again and bounced. Kash must've seen us leave at the same time that day."

"Did ma know?"

"I don't think so." He remained quiet.

"Kruz, I was gonna tell you the day I called your phone but you were busy so I made plans to bring it up later. I got caught up in Sabrina and pushed it to the side. The only reason I came to the hospital is because Zahra sent me a text asking to take a paternity test."

"Why did you come in like, am I the father or uncle? It seemed like you thought it was funny."

"I didn't mean it like that, nor did I want you to find out like that. I think she did it on purpose to hurt you, for not wanting her." I cringed tryna sit up better because the pain was excruciating and I couldn't get comfortable for shit.

"Kruz, we don't see eye to eye, may not be real close but we're close enough that I'd never sleep with your woman. Especially; not one you planned on making your wife." He stared at the ceiling with his hands in his pockets.

"I'm sorry bro. I should've made it my business to tell you as soon as I knew but I didn't know how. And honestly, if a baby wasn't involved, I may not have just to spare you the pain."

"I'm good." He tried to act like it didn't hurt him but I knew better.

"Kruz, I'm your big brother. I know it hurt to hear we slept together because it would've if the situation were reversed."

"Well, everything happens for a reason."

"What you mean?"

"Her cheating brought Rhythm in my life and whether it's been ten years or ten days, I don't see myself with anyone else."

"I would hope so. You married her and she's pregnant."

"Yup."

"There's zero chance that baby is mine." I joked and he snapped his neck.

"Too soon?"

"Way too soon." He leaned down and hugged me without tryna cause pain.

"I love you bro and I'm sorry this happened to you, to us." I told him and meant it. Siblings fight all the time but I never saw us as enemies.

"Love you too." He pulled a chair up next to my bed.

"I'm gonna kill her for instilling all this pain on our family."

"Why is ma trying hard to get y'all back together? Is it a reason she doesn't like Rhythm?" He explained what my mother told him and I was disgusted and sad for her.

No one ever mentioned my father cheating and to hear she degraded herself to deal with the pain, only shows how love hurts and makes you do crazy things. I feel like what she did was a little drastic but I don't know what went through her head either.

"Is it safe to come in now?" Sabrina peeked around the corner.

"Yea." Kruz stood when Rhythm stepped in and brought her closer.

"I didn't get a chance to formally introduce you. Kommon this is my wife Rhythm, and Rhythm, this is my brother Kommon."

"You two definitely look alike." She looked back and forth at us.

"A whole lot. Y'all could be twins." She put her hand on her hips.

"What you talking about? I look way better than him." He grabbed her from behind.

"You cute and all Kruz but you ain't all that."

"I bet this dick is tho. Come sit on it in the bathroom real quick."

"Kruz, stop being nasty." She smacked him on the arm.

"Aren't you the guy who looked into my fraud case?"

"Hold the fuck up. Y'all met before." I could see him getting aggravated.

"Stop getting upset Kruz. Don't nobody want me but you."

"What the hell ever?"

"Anyway. Did you ever find out who the person was that tried to destroy my credit?"

"Ramon never contacted you?" I told him a while back the story but I guess he never took the time out to tell her.

"No."

"Zahra hired some chick she knew from school to do it. They haven't arrested her yet because it's an ongoing investigation. Evidently, she's been doing it for a while."

"Well thank goodness it was caught in time. It's no telling what damage it could've done."

"Don't worry babe. Her time is limited." He sat Rhythm on his lap and we stayed in there talking about any and everything. I'm not even gonna lie; it felt good being around him. I could tell Rhythm brought the best out of him too and that's only after meeting her today.

****

"Are you happy your brother is speaking to you?" Sabrina closed the door, came close, pulled the sheets down and smiled.

Ever since we talked the day after the shooting, he's been here every day. If he didn't come, Rhythm did or Jamaica stopped by. I didn't expect him to because he was shot. But he's like my brother too and regardless of the arguing Kruz and I did, he's still been there if I needed him.

"I am and what are you doing?" She lifted the hospital gown up and started massaging my dick. They took the catheter out a few days ago and I was happy. Who the hell wants to walk around with a colostomy bag?

"You've been in here a while now, which means you have some frustration that needs to be released." Her lips found mine.

"Mmmm." She moaned a little when I stuck my hand in between her legs. All she had on were a pair of sweats that weren't tight so it was easy.

"I love you Kommon." She placed her head on the side of my neck as the orgasm took over. I didn't say anything as she kissed down my chest, skipped my stomach and put me in her mouth. The pain was there because the nut building put strain on it but the feeling is gonna be worth it.

"Oh fuckkkkkk!!!" I yanked her by the hair, pulled her up and forced her face to mine.

"I love you too." She smiled and just as she pulled the gown down and put the sheets back on me, the door opened.

"Are you ok?" My mom rushed in.

This is the first time I've seen her because she was too scared to come up and see Kruz. My father told me after I was shot, she went home and mentioned my brother going off on her about tryna get him with Zahra. He instructed her to give Kruz time to cool off and I guess she listened.

"I'm perfect." I looked at Sabrina and winked. She smiled and went in the bathroom. I could hear the sink going which meant she's cleaning herself up.

"I'm sorry I couldn't be here. Have you eaten?" She opened a bag and pulled a plate of food out.

"Sabrina brings me stuff. What you got?" I sat up and moved the table in front of me.

"Are you hungry Sabrina?" My mom surprised both of us saying that.

"I'm good. Thank you."

"Sabrina, I just want to apologize for how I treated you. I wanted to make sure my son chose the right woman and being you've been here through it all, I'd say he has."

"Thank you for that apology and we can be cordial and respectful to one another. However; Rhythm is my friend and we've become very close. If she's ever around, I won't tolerate you disrespecting her." My mom nodded.

"And for the record, I do understand as a mother you want what's best for your kids. But they are grown men and who they choose is on them."

"I know. Thank you again for taking care of my son when I couldn't."

"I'll be around for a while so get used to seeing me."

"Hell no she ain't going nowhere." I had her sit next to me on the bed as my mother sat on the chair next to it.

She stayed with us for a few hours and even asked Sabrina to stop by whenever she felt like it. I guess after telling

Kruz what Zahra did, she no longer had anything to hold over her head. I was happy as hell too because I got tired of hearing about the shit with Zahra.

"SHIT! Think Zahra." I ran out the hospital fast as hell after shooting Kommon that day. I didn't mean to but from behind he resembled his brother so much, I messed up. Of course, I know the difference but not from the back.

I watched Kommon hit the ground and literally shit on myself when Jamaica pointed his gun at me. Outta nowhere more gunfire went off and it was the best thing that could've happened because I was able to escape down the stairs and out the door. You could hear the hospital going into lockdown but I was too quick.

I flagged down a cab sitting outside, hopped in and regretted setting Mrs. Garcia's car on fire but I had no choice. Plus, I wanted them to believe she was dead. The bitch was supposed to get Kruz and I back together or I'd tell her secret.

See, she cheated on her husband and I caught her because my ass was coming from seeing Kommon. She didn't know that but it wasn't me who got caught.

"Shit, old lady. You sucking the hell out my dick." I *heard walking past an alley. Now me being nosy, I wanted to*

73

see who mother it was this time. Being from the hood nothing
surprises me. I've seen tons of shit in my life but what I walked
up on definitely shocked me.

"Fuck! I'm about to cum." Whoever dude was had his
back against the wall. The woman went to work on him and the
second he pulled out and came, I covered my mouth.

The woman got off her knees, wiped her clothes off, put
her hand out for something and stormed off. He grabbed her
wrist and asked for her phone number. She snatched away and
kept going. I ran to my car and followed the woman to her
house.

"If it isn't Mrs. Garcia." She jumped at my voice and
asked what I wanted. The two of us weren't close but we were
cool.

"Hey honey. I'm in a rush."

"Oh ok." I smirked as she ran inside looking for her
next hit. Instead of saying anything, I kept it to myself. I knew
the information would come in handy one day and it did.

The only thing I didn't bank on was Kruz falling outta love and not want anything to do with me. It's all good because once they find this out she'll be in the doghouse with me.

****

"You have some nerve showing up here." My mother said coming out to her car after work. I could've barged in but her boss threatened to contact the police if I ever returned. I wanted to run away but had no money and Teddy hasn't answered my calls.

"Mommy, I need help."

"You sure do." She kept walking and hit the alarm on her car. I grabbed her.

WHAP! She smacked fire from my ass.

"You bring your trifling ass to my job asking for help after you sent some men there to shoot my house up?" I didn't say anything because she's right.

Teddy and I were up talking one night after fucking and somehow, we got on the subject of Kruz. He found out I'm the one with his daughter and came up with a plan to get him. He wanted revenge for Kruz killing his family members or some shit. But I don't know why after he mentioned robbing him. That's common sense, if you ask me.

I wasn't worried about that because even I knew Kruz wouldn't get caught slipping. My focus was getting Rhythm out the picture. Who knew Teddy didn't care for her either because she didn't wanna give him her number? He's a problem in the making.

Long story short, I told him where my mother lived and the time Rhythm is usually there. Him and some of his people were supposed to shoot up the house, go inside, drag Rhythm out and basically execute her in the street. Clearly, it didn't happen because Rhythm being dead would've been the first thing out her mouth. It's evident I'm gonna have to get her on my own.

"After all I've done for you Zahra, this is how you repay me? By having someone shoot up the house? The kids were there. What if a bullet killed one of them?" I put my head down in shame. I never wanted the kids to be in the middle but if they were there's nothing I can do.

"Your sister and Rhythm had to run out the back. They almost got caught Zahra."

"FUCK RHYTHM!" I shouted and noticed other people coming out to leave.

"Your hatred towards her is sickening."

"You're my mother, not hers. Kalila is my sister and Kenron is my nephew. Why don't you love me the same way you love her?" She opened her car door, threw her purse inside and came towards me.

"You are my child and I love you more than I can say, but your jealousy, hatred and ignorance have this family living in fear."

"Fear?"

"Yes fear? We have no idea who those men are or if they'll return."

"He probably won't come back."

"You don't know that Zahra."

"You're being dramatic."

"Dramatic." She scoffed up a laugh.

"I CAN'T STAY IN MY OWN DAMN HOUSE BECAUSE OF YOU ZAHRA." I folded my arms and leaned against her car. It is my fault she can't go home but so what.

"Then you're jealous of your sisters' best friend because Kalila is closer to her, than you. Do you remember how bad you treated your sister when y'all were young; which is the exact reason why she clung to Rhythm." I rolled my eyes.

"You treated her like shit Zahra. Always hitting her, stealing and breaking her toys, let's not even discuss the time you poured boiling hot water on her when she was seven because you got in trouble. It had nothing to do with Kalila but you took it out on her."

"I was a kid."

"And so was she. Zahra, Rhythm has nothing to do with the sour relationship between you and your sister and you know it. What you need to do is stop blaming her and take responsibility."

"Fuck herrrrrr."

"Zahra why are you trying to destroy anything good coming our way. What is it you want?" I shrugged my shoulders.

"Exactly. You're doing all these hateful things and don't know why."

"I just want Kruz back." I wiped my eyes and noticed the smirk on her face.

"Then you shouldn't have cheated on him, and with his brother Zahra. What were you thinking?"

"I don't even know why. He was perfect for me." I tossed my head back and stared in the sky.

"And now he's perfect for someone else."

"FUCK HER!" I started getting upset all over again.

"I thought you stopped by to apologize but here we are making it all about you." She shook her head.

"Where's my granddaughter?"

"Probably with her father." I said it with no care in the world. I loved my daughter but I'm not mother material.

"I'm sad to say, I've already spoken with a reverend about doing the services for your upcoming funeral."

"What?" Did she know something I didn't? Are they watching me? I began to panic and looked around the parking lot.

"We both know when Kruz, or Jamaica get a hold of you, nothing me or Kalila says, will keep them from taking your life."

"You're just gonna let them kill me?"

"Why wouldn't I? You were gonna let those men kill me and whoever else was in the house." She sat in her car and closed the door.

"What kind of mother are you?"

"The kind who won't deny or hide the foul things my daughter has done. I'm leaving it all in God's hands because I don't know what else to do."

"Ma, please don't leave me to fend for myself." I noticed the tears falling down her face.

"You did this Zahra and you have to face the consequences of your actions."

"Well if I'm dying, so are you?" I pulled the gun out my purse and just as I aimed it at her, she pulled off. I shot as much as I could and watched her car run into a telephone pole.

I guess we'll be in hell together.

I ran off in the other direction hoping no one could point me out before I got in a cab.

"Yes, this is Kalila Bell." I said to the woman on the phone. I didn't know the number but answered anyway.

"Hi. This is the hospital and we have your mother down here."

"My mother?" I was confused because I just spoke to her. She was leaving work to come pick Kenron up and stay at the house. I didn't blame her for not wanting to stay home after the shit my sister pulled. Even Stacey was scared and she lived across the street.

"Yes. She was in a car accident and..."

"I'll be right there." I handed Kenron to his father and went downstairs to the ER. I asked for my mother and a nurse directed me to an area full of cops. I immediately called Jamaica.

"She a'ight?"

"Babe, can you leave lil Kenron with your dad and come down here?" His father has been up here day and night with three of his brothers, who just left an hour ago to change. His two sisters were on their way and don't ask where the other

82

siblings are. He had so damn many I couldn't keep up. His father was not playing when he squirted in his mom.

"Bet." I smiled because he didn't even ask what for. I walked closer to the door and overheard my mother saying Zahra is the one who caused the accident.

"Ma, I know you not in here snitching." I pushed past the officers and stood next to her.

"It's not snitching when it's my own child." I could hear the sadness in her voice.

"She pulled a gun on me Kalila and had I not sped off, you wouldn't have even known I was here for a while because they'd be peeling my brains off the window.

"Ma."

"I'm tired Kalila. If someone doesn't kill her first, she has to go to jail. Otherwise, she's gonna kill me and its not my time to go." I wiped the tears falling down on her face.

"What up?" I heard Jamaica speak and turned around. The detective and cop embraced him in a hug. He moved the crutches to the side of the wall and hopped over to me. The bullets went in his calf and he shouldn't be outta bed but I appreciate him for being here for me.

"You good Ms. Bell?" She covered her face and that's when I knew how embarrassed she was about the things my sister was doing. No parent wants their child to behave the way Zahra does. I keep telling her she did a great job raising us and Zahra chose her own path, but she still blames herself.

"Zahra tried to kill my mother."

"WHAT?" He stared at me and I looked over at the cops who were in their own conversation.

"I don't care who does it, just get it done." He nodded and told my mother everything would be ok, but would it? My sister was doing dumb shit and his ex was just as bad. He still has yet to find her and whoever the guy is she's working with.

"Where's my grandkids?"

"Kenron is upstairs with his granddad, Axel is with his father and I think Kruz's brother has Sasha."

"Jamaica, please make sure someone is watching over them with the kids."

"Kruz hasn't left Rhythm's side and he has someone watching Axel's father's house as well. You know no one can get close to her and you're gonna stay with us until you're ready to go."

"I don't have to."

"Ma, you've been staying with us since she had the house shot up. It's fine."

"I wanna go home."

"You will ma as soon as we catch her. I promise." I kissed her forehead and stepped out with Jamaica.

"I hate seeing her upset." He pulled me in for a hug as he leaned on the wall.

"Kalila, I know it's a lot going on but it will be over soon baby. I promise."

"I believe you." I kissed his lips and asked for a chair so he could sit. The nurse brought one over and I almost cursed her the fuck out for staring hard at my fiancé.

"What I tell you about that fighting shit?"

"Baby, I'm gonna always be protective of this." I pointed to his heart and dick.

85

"I feel the same." We stayed in the ER with my mom until they discharged her.

Evidently; Zahra shot through her back window and it scared my mom. She ran into the telephone pole and banged her head hard on the window. They ran a bunch of tests to make sure nothing else was wrong.

Once they gave her the ok to leave, Jamaica had two of his brothers go home with her to grab some stuff and then to our place. He better hope they find my sister first because if I catch her, I'm gonna beat her to death and I put that on my son.

************************.

"Ok bitch. You in the family now." I joked with Sabrina when I brought Kenron over. Jamaica wanted a night alone and my mom was petrified to watch him at the house.

She was under the assumption Zahra would find her and she couldn't protect him. We told her about the security, the gate won't open without a code and all the other measures Jamaica had in place but she still refused. In my eyes, she assumed Zahra was superwoman or something and could get passed it. I understood her fear though and didn't force her.

When those people came to the house shooting; luckily Rhythm sent a message to Kruz because we may not have made it to book 3. My mom told us some guys snatched her and Stacey up and put them in a car. We didn't know they were ok until we took Rhythm to the hospital and by that time, I was a nervous wreck.

My best friend happened to get hit in the leg by a bullet, my mother and neighbor were fine and unbeknownst to me, my fiancé was at a different hospital in surgery. Shit was all fucked up and, in our case, it led back to my sister. I knew she hated Rhythm but she had to harbor the same towards me if she set it up at my mothers.

Luckily, Jamaica wasn't as bad and came home two days later but it didn't stop him from wanting to kill Zahra for sending me in early labor and shooting Kommon. I was shocked to hear she wished it were Kruz. I guess if she couldn't have him; no one would.

Just like a bitter ex to cause unnecessary drama for no reason. Hey, she did say in the beginning it's how she is. I guess it's never a good thing to underestimate an ex.

For instance, this bitch Kandy is on some other shit too. I haven't told Jamaica but she's reached out threatening to kill me if he doesn't take her back. Text messages and voicemails which are funny because she has an accent. If I didn't know any better I'd say she was pretending to have one. I ain't never heard no Jamaican speak the way she does. The bitch barely gets her words out and stumbles on them.

"Whatever. Give me Kenron." She took him out my arms and walked away.

"What you doing with Axel?"

"TiTi!" He jumped in my arms.

"Axel, you just turned seven a couple months ago. I can't be picking you up like before."

He's small for a seven-year-old but still. His ass is heavy and he always want you to give him a ride on your back or some shit. I blame his father, Rhythm, my mother and now Kruz and Jamaica.

"You're strong now." I sat on the couch and watched Sabrina holding my son. I honestly didn't know we'd get as close because women become intimidated by others and start

88

hating but not us. We all have our own qualities and the men in our lives have no problems reminding us.

"Keep it up and you're next."

"I probably already am."

"Whatttttt?" She smiled.

"Girl when he's not setting up his new business and I'm off, we can't keep our hands off each other. You know how it goes in the beginning of relationships."

"Yea but as long as you keep it spicy and nasty, he ain't going nowhere."

"I hope not."

"Sabrina, most men cheat for whatever reason and the sad part is, the faithful woman at home who's cooking, cleaning and sexing the hell outta them did nothing wrong. I think men have this image to keep of having multiple women. Like it will make them cool to have chicks fighting over them."

"I don't understand the shit."

"Girl, no woman does." We started laughing and I stood to leave.

"Where's mommy Axel?" I hadn't spoken to her all day.

"Home. I wanted to come over." I looked at Sabrina.

"Girl, he goes wherever Kash goes." Just as she mentioned Kash, he was coming down the stairs.

"Assume the position."

"Come on sexy. You know I don't have to steal from my brothers." He had a sneaky grin on his face as he emptied the pockets.

"Stop calling me that." Sabrina rolled her eyes.

"You are sexy."

"This about to be your last time here."

"You like when I call you sexy." She walked over to him.

"I love when my man says it, not a 10-year-old kid. It's inappropriate. Now you may not be scared of Kommon but I know for a fact, your daddy and Kruz don't play that."

"Y'all always running to my dad or brother. Whatever." He waved her off.

"I guess it explains why you're dressed in Kommon's clothes." She had on baggy sweats and a loose fitting hoodie.

"It's the exact reason. I'm not tryna entice nobody's man or child."

"Kash ain't no kid. Don't you know he grown?" I was cracking up.

"Tell her Kalila."

"Boy be quiet."

"I'm serious. When I turn 18, I'm gonna get me a woman as fine as you two."

"Ain't no chick gonna want a damn klepto."

"Klepto? Kalila please. I ain't stole nothing in a while." Sabrina and I looked at each other and busted out laughing.

"You shouldn't have been stealing at all."

"I'ma tell you like I tell my family, *if people didn't want their things stolen why would they leave it out? Especially; when they know I'm around. They know I may or may not take it, so why chance it.*" He shrugged his shoulders and sat next to Axel.

"That makes no sense Kash. If people leave things out it's not an invitation to take it."

"Sure it is." I couldn't go on anymore with him because it's clear he sees no wrong in his actions. I said my goodbyes, kissed my son and went home to my man.

I lit the candles when Kalia mentioned she was in the parking lot of the condo, we owned. I say we, because she's been on all my paperwork for a while. I haven't told her every aspect of the businesses I owned and other things, but she's aware.

We came here because even though we can fuck in the house, I wanted to show her how much I appreciate everything she's done. Most women would've left dealing with an ex who tried to get her and her man killed but my girl is right here y my side.

Call me corny all you want but a woman wants a nigga to continue treating her the same as when they first met.

I heard the door unlock and walked over to greet her. When she opened it, I noticed the smile gracing her face. I held her hand, closed the door and led her upstairs to the bathroom where I put rose petals in the tub. She loved that shit. She tried to remove her clothes but I took over and told her, its my job to take care of her tonight.

I trailed kisses down her neck, unbuttoned the shirt she had on and smiled at the sexy bra. Kalila never wore ugly bra sets and I loved staring at her body in them.

"Get in ma." I said after taking the rest of her clothes off. As she sat, I grabbed the bottle of wine in the bucket, and poured her a glass.

"Babe, you tryna get your dick sucked real good tonight." I busted out laughing and almost spilled the drink.

"There's never been a time when it wasn't good." I winked and handed her the glass.

"You joining me?"

"Nah, because I wanna make love to you all over and that tub tight as hell."

"Jamaica." I shushed her with a kiss and went in the bedroom to turn the music on.

After about twenty minutes, I walked back in the bathroom to see her dosing off. I turned the hot water on, grabbed the sponge to wash her and carried her in the room. Staring down at Kalila made me realize she is the only woman I see myself with and its not because of her body.

94

She's smart, beautiful, can fuck me straight to sleep and most importantly, takes very good care of me and my son. How I could hurt her is beyond me but it won't happen again. Those two months without her were torture and I don't wanna deal with that again. Men can play the *I don't give a fuck she left role* all they want but my ass was stuck.

I placed a kiss on her lips, moved down to her breasts and began sucking on one of them. I tugged on one of her nipples and heard a slight moan escape her lips. Each time I flickered her sensitive nipples she let out a soft moan. She started thrusting her hips against my sweats, I had yet to remove. I move my hands down her body, pull my dick out and tease her clit with the tip. Her body shuddered and she tried to scoot down on it.

"You want this K?"

"Yessss baby. I want it."

"I'ma give it to you but I wanna taste that pussy first." I looked up to see her shaking her head and biting down on her lip.

I pressed my tongue on her already protruding clit and took a long and slow lick. She pushed her pussy down on my face and started grinding her hips. I gripped her ass to give myself more access to her treasure and dove right in. Each time my tongue assaulted her clit, I could see her getting closer to the edge. The orgasm was coming up fast and we both knew it.

"Ohhhhh fuckkkkkk Kenron." I watched it tear through her body and send her into a state of shock.

Her body jerked and instead of waiting on her to finish, I lapped up all her juices and, in the process gave her more orgasms then she's ever had. I kissed the inside of her thighs and smiled at her lying there tryna catch her breath.

"Baby, I just wanna go to sleep." She attempted to roll over but I moved her body closer to mine.

"We ain't done ma." I intertwined her hands in mine and lifted her up.

"Fine!" She pushed me away from the bed, got on her knees and took me in her mouth. I watched the saliva drip from her mouth, as she bobbed her head up and down. The intense feeling was starting to overwhelm me and I tried holding it in.

"Oh shit K. Fuckkkkk." I couldn't hold out any longer and gave her what she asked for.

I lifted her up, put her on all fours and ate her ass and pussy until she begged me to stop. I rolled on my back, had her climb on top and put my hands behind my head as she rocked slowly on my dick. She moved up to the tip, then dropped hard so her pussy could flush against my skin. Her clit was grinding against me, her titites were bouncing up and down and her sexy ass jiggled the entire time.

I wrapped my hands around her waist and fucked the shit outta her from underneath. I buried myself deeper and deeper to make sure she felt me.

"Kenron, I'm about to. Oh my Goddddddd!" Her nails dug in my chest as I continued pulverizing the pussy. I flipped her over, opened her ass cheeks and fucked her hard, then slow and hard again. Both of us were moaning and enjoying the moment.

"When you gonna be my wife?" I had her hair in my hand as I hit it from behind.

"Whenever you're ready. Don't stop." She started throwing her ass back and both of us came at the same time. I collapsed on her back. Sweat was all over both of us and my dick was still inside.

"That was amazing baby." She maneuvered from under me and kissed my lips.

"We just getting started ma." She smiled.

"It's gonna be a long night."

"As long as you know." The two of us went back at it and after cumming a lot we passed out naked and satisfied.

****

"What up nigga? Damn, Kalila did that to your neck?" I gave Kruz a look.

"I'm just saying. I ain't never seen her leave one on you."

"Like my ass would be allowed in the house or even alive if another bitch did it."

"Touché."

"Anyway. What's up with Zahra?"

"Not a damn thing. I don't have a clue where she's at and really don't care now that my daughter's back."

"I hear ya."

"Oh, I'm gonna kill her if you don't get her first, but my main concern is the family and this bullshit with Kandy. Have you heard anything from her?" He said looking down on his phone.

"Nah but you know that means nothing." Me, him, and the team stepped on my jet and flew to California. Its where her sister lived and if I was gonna find her, it's time for me to bring her outta hiding. Her father claims to be tryna assist in anything I need to get her but it's funny how he supposedly hasn't seen her either.

At first, I didn't think much of it because he's never lied to me. That is until I ran into his wife, and she told me a different story. Unbeknownst to her, she assumed her husband was on the same team and informed me of Kandy stopping by a few times.

She could care less if the bitch died or not because they've gotten into it on plenty of occasions. Evidently; Kandy wanted her parents back together and voiced her opinion in front of the wife, who had no issue kicking her out.

The night my father showed me the evidence he had of Kandy's mom being involved in the untimely death of my mother, I was livid. There were photos of my mother shopping, out with my father, and doing things around the house. Only someone who's stalking would have these photos.

Anyway, there were emails to some guy who set up the bank robber job and the most important thing, was the fact she stood there as the robbers ran out the bank with a smile on her face. We only saw her there because of the surveillance video.

Long story short, my father said she was mad he didn't talk his best friend into getting her in the states. She went to my father for assistance and since he didn't help her, she thought he should suffer. It was a dumb ass reason to have my mother killed but I guess when you really want something you go to extreme measures to get it.

The crazy thing is, she's still in Guyana and can't get here. What I don't understand is why she couldn't come here? I mean, why didn't she just sign up for another green card or something? I guess it's one thing I'll never know because while I'm here to take her kids out, my father is on his way with my brothers to kill her.

"We here." Kruz tapped me on the shoulder and brought me out the zone I was in. I sent Kalila a text and told her I'd be home tonight.

"You ready?"

"Yup."

We stepped off the jet and walked to the black truck waiting. It's good to have a jet because you can bring whatever you want on it. When I tell you, we had tons of weapons, we really did. Mr. Euburne had his daughter protected and for good reason. He had and still has tons of enemies but it comes with the territory.

The truck stopped a block away from the mansion Kandy's sister lived in. We got out, put on our vest and proceeded with caution. If anyone knew how we rolled it was always reckless, yet; safe. When I say reckless, I mean more of not giving a fuck about who gets hurt in the process and dealt with any consequences later.

PHEW! PHEW! PHEW! PHEW! TATTTTTTTTT!

TATTTTTT! We went in with our guns blazing. Bodies were

dropping like flies and so did two Pitbull's on the property.

"Hello Margie." She turned around in the kitchen and

wiped her hands on the apron. The guys were canvasing the

house to make sure no one else was in there. I heard a few

shots here and there and assumed this house was contaminated

with multiple henchmen or whatever you wanna call them.

"How are you Jamaica? I've been expecting you."

"That's good to know. Where's your sister?"

"Unfortunately, I don't know where the ungrateful

whore is, but I do know if she has you murdering people on my

property, you have no idea where she is either." I cocked my

gun and aimed it at the guy standing in the closet.

BOOM! I cocked the shotgun again and pulled the

trigger as another man emerged from the pantry.

"How many more?" She had her hands covering her

mouth.

"Ummmm." She started walking backwards and feeling for something, which only lead me to believe she also had a weapon somewhere.

"One more time." I put two bullets in the shotgun as she continued moving around the kitchen.

"Where's Kandy?" She stopped when her body hit the wall. I lifted the gun, placed it on her forehead and waited for the answer.

"Please don't kill me." I cocked it.

"MY FATHER HAS HER HIDDEN SOMEWHERE IN HIS HOUSE. THERE'S A SECRET PASSAGEWAY INSIDE AND NO ONE KMOWS ABOUT IT; NOT EVEN HIS WIFE."

"Which house?" I questioned because we both knew he had various ones in different states.

"The one in Delaware."

"Where's the boyfriend Geoffrey?"

"He's with her."

"Thanks for the info but your father should've protected you better."

"Huh?"

BOOM! Her brains were all over the kitchen wall. I moved away and walked upstairs to where the guys were.

"What you wanna do with this?" It was a black safe inside the wall. It wasn't too big but not small either.

"Let's see what's in it." One of the guys shot it up until it opened and money fell out. I had them place it in a bag and told them they can split it up. It's their payment for coming.

Drew came in pouring gasoline all over the house, as I went in the office and removed all the security footage along with laptops, any USB cable and whatever else I thought would be of use.

"Hell yea, I'ma tear that pussy up when I get home."

"Nigga are you seriously on the phone with yo wife talking about fucking?" He turned around with a grin on his face.

"Hell motherfucking yea. I know ain't nobody doing nothing in here." I laughed at his strung out ass.

"Bye Rhythm." I shouted and he sucked his teeth.

"A'ight ma. I'll be there soon." He hung up and put the phone up.

"You stay hatin."

"What the fuck ever. My fiancé will defiantly be waiting when I get home."

"Y'all two done going back and forth? We need to set this place on fire and get outta here." Drew stood there with a lighter in his hand. All of us stepped out and walked away as the house exploded. Time to go home.

"Hey lil mama." I picked Sasha up out her crib. It was after midnight, and I just walked in the house. After we handled the shit in California, we came straight home. However; with the time difference, it was later here.

"You're gonna stay up with her if she wakes up." I heard Rhythm behind me and put her back in the crib.

"I mean how are you gonna be able to handle this if you're tryna get her back to sleep?" I turned around and my wife had on a sheer robe, with some heels on.

"How you walking around naked with kids here?" I was talking about Axel and my nasty ass brother who damn near lived here now. He was here all the time.

"Axel is with his father and Kash has a crush on Sabrina so he's been staying there."

"Is that right?"

"It is but if you don't wanna handle this tonight, we can wait until you're ready." She went to turn and I had to calm my dick down. Her ass sat up right and it didn't help she bent over to pick up a toy, which gave me access to her pussy spread wide open.

"You love playing."

"Who's playing?" She smirked and gestured me with her finger to follow. I went behind and smiled when we stepped in the room. The lights were red, and so were the candles and sheets.

"What's all this?"

"Can't I do something nice for my husband?" She pressed the button to the stereo sound and Red-Light Special came on by TLC.

"DAMN!" My wife started to do a strip tease for me and I couldn't get my clothes off fast enough.

After the song went off, she stood in front of me fully exposed. At five and a half months pregnant, Rhythm was still beautiful as ever in my eyes. I kissed her belly a few times and let two of my fingers roam down to her soaking wet pussy. The first moan made my dick even harder as I worked them in and out. My thumb circled her enlarged clit at the same time. Her head fell back and her lower half began to succumb to my fingers.

"Oh fuck Kruz." She shook and exploded.

I stood and closed the space between us. I could feel her nipples against my chest, which made them harden. I grabbed her chin gently and separated her lips with my tongue. As our tongues explored one another, I could feel her soft hands stroking me. She pushed me away, scooted on the bed and smiled.

"Kruz, I want you to fuck me."

"Oh yea."

"Yea and I'm not talking about just putting it in and going hard. I want you fucking my titties, my mouth, pussy and anywhere else you desire." I licked my lips listening to her describe how she wanted it. Women will show you by the way they move their bodies but I loved hearing her tell me.

"You sure you can handle all that with my baby in you?"

"I think so." She smirked and spread her legs open. Her fingers rubbed over her clit slowly.

"Kiss me Kruz." I climbed on the bed, and gave her one. I cupped one of her breasts and felt her body shudder. I moved her hands out the way and replaced them with mine. She began grinding under me and her pearl became harder.

"Oh my God it feels so good baby. Don't stop." Her body began bucking as the orgasm took over. I got off the bed, grabbed her down by the ankles and in one thrust, I was inside.

"I'm cumming again Kruz. Fuckkk!" I let her legs go and she locked them behind my back. The more I pumped, the more our body became in sync.

There's no doubt in my mind that I made the right choice in choosing her as my wife. It felt like we were meant to be together.

"That was incredible baby." Rhythm said in between breaths. She and I had been at it most of the night and we were both worn out.

"It's always incredible; what you talking about?" I spooned her naked body from behind and rested my arm on her stomach.

"Sometimes it's boring."

"WHAT?" I forced her to look at me.

"I'm just kidding." She put her hands on the side of my face.

"Every time with you is like a new experience. I love the things you do to my body."

"You better or I'll have to find some other chick to appreciate this good dick."

"And you and her will end up in a ditch somewhere bleeding from your skull."

"You know terroristic threats hold up in court."

"So does insanity." She shrugged and made herself comfortable under my arm. I guess, I did find someone that's crazy over me, as I am for them.

God don't make mistakes so me finding out about my ex was meant to be. Rhythm just happened to be the woman I crossed paths with when we broke up.

In the beginning, my plans were to fuck every chick in sight and it's exactly what I did. Then, Rhythm and I started texting and talking on the phone. The conversations were fun and intellectual at times. Overall, she made it easy for me to talk and didn't judge me on the past or the things I do; not that she knows everything but still.

****

"Why are you here?" My mom had a panicked look on her face. I had my brother Kommon meet me here so we can discuss what she told me.

"One... our parents live here and two... you're gonna have to elaborate more on the past." I gave her a fake smile and stepped in to see my father zipping his pants up. I looked at her and then him.

"Yuk." Kommon shook his head laughing.

"Boy, your mother got some good stuff..."

"Then why did you cheat on her?" He glanced at my mom who instantly started to cry.

"Tha hell you crying for?"

"It's in the past Kruz and I still get upset thinking about it."

"This nigga had you doing crackhead shit in alleyways and you're telling me it's in the past."

111

"Kruz, I don't give a fuck about how those niggas on the street are scared of you. When you in this motherfucking house, you respect everyone in it; unless we put our hands on you."

My father was in my face and I could care less about the bass in his voice. At the end of the day, she's my mother and he had no business cheating. Especially; when he told us not to do it to our own women.

"Kruz, let's have a seat and hear what he has to say." Kommon pushed me back and I could see pain on his face. He may be up and moving around but the shooting took a toll on his body.

"What the fuck ever." I moved to the loveseat and my mother sat across from me with my father. No one said a word and I could tell my pops was struggling to mention it.

"Why did you step out on ma?" Kommon asked.

"It's no real reason why."

"Then why you do it?" The tone in my voice was aggressive and again, I didn't care.

"The woman from the post office who delivered the mail used to flirt with me all the time. I never paid her any mind until she caught me out at the bar one night. She came on stronger and instead of denying her advance, we ended up in a hotel room." I saw the tears running down my mother face and felt bad. Maybe I shouldn't have brought it up in front of her.

"The affair went on for a few months. The night I tried to end it, we had sex and it's when she mentioned a pregnancy."

"How you get another bitch pregnant tho?"

"Nigga, you got one more time and son or not, we'll be squaring up in this bitch." My father knew he pumped no fear in my heart. Shit; he's the one who made me the way I am.

"Just stop it." My mom grabbed his hand and waited for him to finish telling his side.

"I honestly don't know how she got pregnant because I was always protected."

"Who brought the condoms?" Kommon asked the question in my head.

"We took turns why?" We both shook our heads. Everyone knows you don't trust a bitch to bring them. Especially, one who's been tryna fuck knowing you had a woman.

"Anyway, your mom caught us and it tore me up to see her hurting." My mom stared at him with adoration and I had no fucking idea why.

"She disappeared for two days and I was sick. All I could think about was if she got hurt or in an accident. She didn't answer my calls and I couldn't find her. Long story short; when she did come home, I had already taken the chick to get an abortion and broke things off. Your mother was still hurt though and I could see it all over her face."

"It's over now son and we dealt with it in our own way."

"Let me get this straight." I scooted to the edge of the loveseat and rested my elbows on my knees.

"He cheated on you, you acted like a crackhead for a minute, y'all get over it and move on."

"It's not as easy as you make it sound but your father and I have way too much time in to let some woman destroy our union."

"Oh, you're just gonna skip over the fact you had some man's dick in your mouth? Knees probably fucked up and shit from the asphalt and rocks." My mother sucked her teeth and Kommon laughed hard as hell.

"Where's the guy?

"Why do you wanna know?"

"Pops, I can't have no nigga out here saying my moms sucked him off for drugs. He needs to be dealt with." My father picked his cigar up, lit it and blew smoke in the air.

"He'll never see the light of day again." My mom snapped her neck and I smirked.

"Kommon Sr. Do not tell me you killed him."

"Ok. I won't." He shrugged his shoulders.

"How did you even know who he was or what happened?" He blew smoke again.

"After you couldn't be found those two days, I made it my business to know where you are at all times." She covered her mouth.

"The person watching you called and said, you walked in an alley with some guy. By the time I got there you were leaving." She put her head down.

"I may not have witnessed you in the act but I know something went down because he was zipping his jeans up." None if us said a word.

"Anyway, he hopped in his car, I followed and bumped his car from behind. He pulled over, started popping shit on the side of the road, I shot him in the head a few times and came home." Kommon and I looked at each other and back at him.

"You know, to this day that case is still unsolved. Hmmm. Go figure." I had to respect the game. My OG wasn't with the shits and made sure no one ever found out.

"Well I guess I should kill the woman you were with." She folded her arms across her chest.

"She was dead the same night I took her to get an abortion."

"KOMMON!"

"What? At least I didn't kill the child." He got up and walked out on the porch.

"All the men in this family are crazy, except Kash."

"You damn right he ain't crazy because he's a got damn thief. By the way, did you ever retrieve your laptop?" She sucked her teeth and walked away. Kash could do no wrong in her eyes. I made my way on the porch and took a seat next to my father.

"Shit is all the way fucked up."

"I know son and I'm sorry she let that bitch blackmail her. Had she mentioned it, we may have been able to catch her."

"Yea. At least Sasha is safe and the doctor said, she thinks Zahra let her fall off the bed."

"You need to find her quick."

"I'm trying but wherever she is or whoever's hiding her is doing a damn good job."

"You have to do better than them. Think of all the places she may go or ever wanted to go. Hell, she could be right here in town and we'd never know."

"Yea." I laid my head back on the seat.

"And don't ever bring your ass up in my shit, acting like I won't go upside your fucking head." He sounded aggressive but I expected it because this is his house and he had every right to react this way.

"You're right and I apologize. I was upset ma had to stoop that low to get your attention or to get that high."

"I know and I get sick all over every time I think about what my infidelity did to her." He passed me his cigar and the two of us sat out there discussing other shit. Kommon came out and said he had to go because he was feeling pain. I promised my mother I'd take care of him and I have been but his ass don't listen when you tell him to take it easy.

"How did it go at your mom's?" Kruz stopped by my job on the way to the house. He went to see his parents earlier to discuss the foul crap she did.

"Crazy. My pops killed the woman he cheated on her with, and the nigga whose dick she got caught sucking."

"KRUZ!"

"What? Shit, she was being a fiend. I bet she had cuts and shit on her knees from the rocks." I was cracking up.

"You know why she did it so give her a break."

"Hell no. All she had to do is tell us. Instead, she had that bitch back, and look what happened. My daughter had a knot on her head, she had her mom's house shot up, tried to kill her nephew and let's not forget she tricked me at the doctor's office." I turned my head from the computer and looked at him. He was stuffing his face with some Chinese food.

"Tricked you?"

"Damn right." He poured soy sauce on his shrimp roll.

"How you figure?" I folded my arms.

119

"She knows I like my dick sucked and since she learned how to do it, she tried it on me." He shrugged his shoulders, like the shit he said made sense.

"Nigga, you didn't have to let her close to you at all."

"It happened so fast though Rhythm. Maybe she was a vampire or something."

"A vampire, really? Kruz stop blaming her and take responsibility for your part on it."

"Nope. Can't do it."

"Why not?"

"Because then I'd admit to cheating on you and being wrong and I'm not admitting to nothing."

"But you did."

"You have no proof. You're only going off what she said."

"Are you serious? Kruz, you just said she sucked you off because she knew you liked it."

"I did?"

"Ugh, yea you did." He gave me a weird look.

"You focus on the past too much."

"You just said it five minutes ago."

"Exactly! The past. Let's move on." I swear he was a piece of work but I loved everything about him, even if it meant he said stupid shit from time to time.

I sat back down at the desk and looked over the rooms and noticed one of them hasn't been paid for in two weeks. How is the room still considered non-vacant if there's no payment on file? I could say the owner knows the person but the only people I'm aware he's lets do whatever is my husband and friends. I picked the keys up to the room and headed towards the door.

"Where you going?" He came out the bathroom and wrapped his arms around my waist.

"I have to see why this room isn't vacant when no one is paying the bill."

"When you gonna stop working Rhythm?" He held my hand in his and we stepped out the office together.

"Why would I leave? The owner gave me a job straight outta high school and has helped me a lot."

121

"You're married now and there's no reason for my wife to be working." He turned his nose up at the place.

"I'll buy a lot and let you open your own motel but I don't want you working here anymore."

"You don't have to buy me anything baby."

"Rhythm you know what goes on here and I refuse to let you be around it anymore." We stopped and he had me face him.

"I'm not tryna control you or make you lose your independence but we both know your husband is rich, which means you are. Use some money to open up something."

"Can I open a strip club?" I smirked.

"Yup and I'll be the first customer. But yo ass ain't stepping on no stage."

"I think my stripper skills are good. What you think?" I pushed him against the wall a few doors down from the room I need to check and ran my hand up his chest.

"They are very good but it's for my eyes only." He placed his hands under my shirt and sent chills down my spine by the way he touched. I let a soft moan out because it felt so good.

"Look at you tryna fuck. This what I'm talking about. Never working anyway so you may as well quit."

"You always talking shit, you know that."

"And you curse a lot for someone who said they didn't when we first met."

"I can't help it around you." I backed away and went to walk to the room, when the door opened and out walked this bitch.

CLICK! Kruz was fast with his weapon out but she was faster and pointed it at my stomach.

"Get behind me Rhythm."

"Kruz she's not gonna shoot me."

"Oh no bitch. I'm gonna kill that bastard in your stomach." She cocked the gun back.

"No you won't and I'm gonna tell you why." I moved closer and her hands were shaking.

"Because the second you fire a shot, you'll be dead and we both know it because my husband won't allow you to take another step."

"Husband?" She started walking backwards.

"I swear delusional women never hear everything when it comes to a man they can't get over."

"Rhythm, get behind me."

"Put the gun away Zahra because there's nowhere to run." I held my hands up.

"Fuck you." Her finger moved on the trigger and Kruz pushed me outta the way.

BOOM! She fired off and Kruz fell on the side of the wall.

"I'm gonna get you bitch." I grabbed the gun out his hand and ran down the steps as fast as I could. She hopped in some car and I let off every bullet in the gun. I heard her scream and the windows were shattered. Unfortunately, I didn't get the tires; therefore, she was able to pull off.

I went back up the steps to check on Kruz. He was holding his arm and telling me to get his phone and call

Jamaica. I did like he asked and had him go in the room with me. He scooted inside and to say we were shocked is an understatement. There were baby clothes, diapers, food, a bassinet and other things that belonged to a baby. I grabbed some papers off the bed and it was to get a passport. This bitch was about to skip town, well try because Kruz isn't gonna let her.

"Shit, you're bleeding bad." I pointed to his shoulder. I took his belt off and tied it around his arm. I tried to call the ambulance but he wouldn't let me. I guess we had to wait for Jamaica and whoever else to get here.

****

"How you feeling baby?" We were at the house after leaving the hospital. Jamaica and Drew came and took him there. They didn't want the ambulance coming to the motel because then it would cause them to look into the rooms and no one wanted that.

"Did you know she was staying at the hotel?" Jamaica, Kalila, Drew, Kommon and his father all looked at him. I think

125

we were all shocked he even had the audacity to ask me some shit like that.

"Excuse me!"

"You heard me. Did you know she was staying there?"

"How could you ask me something like that?"

"You work at the motel five days a week Rhythm. You mean to tell me; not once did you see her or my daughter."

WHAP! I smacked the shit outta him and everyone jumped up when he hopped out the bed.

"Don't ever in your fucking life put your hands on me again." I noticed his fists were balled up.

"Oh, I'm supposed to be scared now? What you gonna do?"

"If you weren't pregnant?"

"If I weren't pregnant what?" I didn't back down from him.

"You know Kruz, you're not the only one who suffered when she took Sasha. You're not the only one who was hurt over all the stupid shit she was doing. You're accusing me of harboring that bitch knowing she had your daughter. Yet; you

126

standing here mad at the person who said in front of your mother, that I'd kill her if I saw her."

"Unless I put my hands on you, don't ever put your fucking hands on me again." It's like he ignored everything I said to focus on me hitting him.

"Rhythm, maybe we should go. Both of y'all are upset and..." Kalila stood in front of me.

"You're right sis. I mean, why would I wanna be around a man who thinks I'd keep his daughter away from him too?" Kruz remained in the same spot and I could see a little bit of blood trickling out the bandage on his shoulder. I picked my purse up, said my goodbyes to everyone and walked to the door.

"Oh wait!" I looked down at my ring and started crying immediately.

"I want a divorce." Everyone looked surprise and nervous for me at the same time.

"Get tha fuck out my face Rhythm." I put the ring on the bed and noticed him walking closer to me. This time he was angrier and a hint of sadness seeped through.

"I refuse to be married to a man who thinks I'd keep his own daughter from him. I love you Kruz but this ain't gonna work. Goodbye." I wiped my face and backed up. By now, he was very angry and it definitely scared me.

"Look." His father stood.

"Both of you are upset and we all get it. Kruz you're accusing her of something because you're mad. Rhythm you're upset and smacked him and we get it but a word of caution when it comes to my son." He walked to where I was as Kruz and I stared each other down.

"I'm not saying he was right for even asking you that bullshit but you had no business putting your hands on him." I broke the stare and put my head down. I never wanted to be a woman who laid hands on her man.

"Anyone else would've already been gone and I think you know that." He lifted my face.

"You two need to stay away from one another until things cool off because I can't guarantee he won't react differently, if you smack him again."

"We'll have all the break we need because I'm filing for a divorce in the morning." I hurried out before he could catch me with Kalila on my heels.

"FUCK!" I shouted out to no one in particular as I drove this shot up car to Teddy. The bitch got me in the back of my leg when I closed the door.

I only stopped by the motel to pick up a few things because I knew time was of the essence. I had to skip town and fast. I knew once my sister found out about my mother she'd be added to the list of people who wanted me.

I gathered as much as possible to leave and peeked out the window. I've been here all this time without getting caught so I figured today wouldn't be an issue. What I didn't expect is to see those fake ass lovebirds feeling each other up.

Shock was evident on their faces but what surprised me is the bitch calling Kruz her husband. We were together all those years and I didn't even get a got damn promise ring. How the fuck did he marry her ugly ass and never proposed to me?

Hell yea I was pissed, which is exactly why I pointed my gun at her stomach. The only thing stopping me from pulling the trigger was the fact I could possibly miss and Kruz

130

would kill me. If that happened how would I know the bitch suffered?

When she continued moving forward I panicked and shot anyway. I caught Kruz because he jumped in front of her. The bitch definitely chased after me and would've caught my ass had she not been pregnant. Whatever the case I'm glad I got away that's for sure.

"What the hell happened to you?" Teddy shouted when I stepped in his sister's house. He's been laying low since I had him and his friends shoot up my mother's place. I wasn't tryna kill the kids but my sister, Rhythm and anyone else could die for all I care.

"I tried to get out the motel quick but they were there." He hopped up and ran to the window.

"Who was there?" He peeked out the curtain.

"What the hell happened to the car?" I explained what went down and he shook his head.

"Teddy, she shot me in the leg an all you're worried about is your damn car."

"Bitch, I don't care about your fucking leg. What I care about is the fact you drove the motherfucker here. What if someone followed your stupid ass?"

"No one followed me because I shot Kruz." He stopped pacing and stared.

"Did he die?"

"I don't know fool; I ran."

"You have to be the dumbest bitch I know."

"Stop calling me a bitch and can you get me a towel or find someone to help me?

"Nobody told your stupid ass to leave the scene without making sure everyone was dead. AND STOP BLEEDING ALL OVER MY SISTER HOUSE." He shouted and threw a towel in my face. I grabbed it and pressed down on my leg. It didn't stop the pain and the fact I was feeling dizzy.

Teddy was on the phone in the other room yelling about someone coming to help. I hope they hurry up because this shit hurts. I don't understand how people get shot and then brag like it's cute.

"My boy's girlfriend is a nurse. He bringing her by now."

"Good."

"Let's go out in the garage." I put my hand out for him to help and he kept walking.

"TEDDY!"

"WHAT?"

"I need help."

"You made it here. You can make it to the garage."

"Are you serious?"

"Hell yea I'm serious. Bad enough I'm the one who has to clean all the blood up before my sister gets here." I sucked my teeth and struggled to get out in the garage. Once I did, I sat in a chair and waited for the guy to come. He has the worst hospitality ever.

****

"You are some kinda crazy bringing your ass around me." Mrs. Garcia said outside the grocery store.

"Can we talk?" She placed some bags in her trunk and slammed it down.

"First, I wanna apologize for cursing at you in the hospital."

"Keep going." She waved her hand in the air telling me to hurry up without words.

"I should've never taken my anger out on you and thanks for going to get her. Where is she by the way?"

"You didn't have to ask." She went on to tell me Kruz had her and it pissed me off because he's married to Rhythm, which means she's raising my child.

"Anything else?" She unlocked her car door.

"I know it's a lot to ask but can you bring Sasha to your house so I can see her?"

"How the hell are you going to come over my house?"

"You can send your husband to the store or something. Please Mrs. Garcia. I miss her." I gave her the best cry I could get out at the moment. It took her a few seconds to agree and I was happy like a pig in shit when she did.

I may not be mother material but the only way to hurt Kruz at this point is to take his most prized possession away.

It's not like he'll be too upset because he has another one on the way.

"Thank you. Thank you."

"Where are you staying?" I looked at her crazy. Does she really think I'll tell her where?

"When's the last time you spoke to your son?"

"I haven't spoken to him since he found out about my infidelity."

"How did he find out because I haven't spoken a word." Shit, if he knows I don't have any leverage against her.

"I had to tell him because he was threatening to keep my grandchild away." I could hear how upset it made her to speak on it.

"Have you become acquainted with Rhythm?"

"Nope and I don't plan on it. You know they got married and didn't invite me?"

"Wow! I guess she's turning him against his family huh? Something I'd never did or would do."

"I know sweetie and trust me when I say, I tried my hardest to get you two back together. He wouldn't budge."

135

"I know. She threw herself at him and rushed to get pregnant to keep him around."

"It's crazy." She shook her head.

"Let me go. I'll contact you when Sasha comes over. Do you have the same number?"

"No. I had to get a prepaid. This is the number." I read it off and hopped back to my car. I couldn't wait to get my daughter and leave. This time I'm never coming back.

I watched her pull off and thought to myself if she setting me up, I'm gonna kill her. What am I saying? She'd never do that. I smiled to myself and pulled off awaiting her call.

"Bitch, it's been two days. Are you still not talking to him?" I asked Rhythm at lunch.

After the fiasco her and Kruz went through no one has really spoken to either of them. She refused to stay in the big house and went to the one in Sayreville. He went home and Jamaica said he hasn't even mentioned anything about the divorce or her. He's been spending time with Sasha and Axel who wanted to stay at the house with him because Kash was always there. I had to laugh because he never stayed without his mom and now he's always with his stepdad.

"Nope and I'm fine. What you ordering?" She picked the menu up and I smacked it down.

"Heffa, it's me you're talking to. I know good and well you're hurting and want your man back. Both of you are stubborn as fuck, which has me and my fiancé stuck in the middle tryna get y'all back on the same page."

"He was ready to kill me Kalila. I don't need a man like that."

"Are you seriously pretending not to know why?"

137

"I'm a woman and…"

"Exactly! A woman who knew good and damn well how her husband is. Best friend or not, Rhythm you were dead ass wrong for smacking him and you know it."

"So that means he gets to hit me?"

"He didn't hit you Rhythm and he said not to do it again."

"Ok, the fact he even made the threat is enough."

"Rhythm, what's wrong with you? You of all people have never swung on a man unless necessary." She just broke down crying.

"My hormones are acting up and he pissed me off thinking I would keep Zahra hidden from him. Does he really think that low of me?"

"I don't know why he asked and I'm gonna say it again. You had no business hitting him."

"I know and I wanted to apologize but he jumped up and I wasn't backing down. Who the fuck he think, he is?" I shook my head laughing. One minute she saying he should've never accused her of anything and then wanted to say sorry.

"Girl, you better suck his dick from behind or something because its gonna take a lot to make up for that shit." We both started laughing and waved the waitress over. She took our orders and walked away. I slid closer to her and went through the wedding dresses I liked.

"Oh, hell no!" I followed the direction Rhythm was looking and blew my breath in the air. This is gonna be some shit. I sent a text to Jamaica and asked him to come here.

Kruz stepped in with some light skinned woman who resembled Alicia Keys. She had on a pant suit with heels and her hair was braided up in dreads. She wore minimal makeup and seemed to have all of his attention. I could see my girl tearing up and felt bad but not too bad because she brought this on herself. Let alone we have no idea who the chick is.

"Stay calm Rhythm."

"What up?" He stopped at our table.

"Not much. Who is this?" I pointed to the woman who now had her face engrossed in her phone.

"This is Mrs. Reynolds; my divorce lawyer." I covered my mouth and Rhythm nodded her head.

"Well let her know I'm gonna take half of yo shit and I want custody of Sasha." He snatched Rhythm up out the chair.

"I play a lotta fucking games but you're about to walk on dangerous grounds and when I say no one will be able to save you, they won't."

"Is that a threat?"

"You know me better than that Rhythm." He let her shirt go and backed away.

"Keep playing this game you know, you're gonna lose and I'm gonna be the one raising Axel. Fuck with me if you want." He put up a peace sign an escorted the woman to a seat.

"You are not taking my son."

"Think again." He smirked. Rhythm snatched her stuff up and stormed out the restaurant.

"He's not taking my son Kalila."

"You mentioned taking his daughter, what did you expect?"

"Bitch, whose side you on?" She wiped her eyes and stared at me.

"Yours but you're wrong and you know it." She sucked her teeth and walked ahead of me.

"Give me your keys." She had her hand out. I passed them to her and watched as the trunk popped open.

"What you about to do?" She removed the metal bat and walked to the parking lot. When she got to his truck, I closed my eyes.

CRASH! There goes the driver's side window.

"Bitch, are you crazy? You know how much he loves this truck."

"Too fucking bad."

CRASH! CRASH! CRASH! CRASH! She took out the rest of the window and walked to the windshield. It took a few more hits and the windshield caved in.

She opened the door and used my key to try and cut up the seats. It did a little damage but not too much. She closed it and literally dragged it all around his truck. I thought about stepping in but what kind of friend would I be if I didn't let her get out the frustrations?

I took my phone out and took photos of the damage. If he wasn't gonna kill her before, he will now.

"A'ight bitch, that's enough."

"Not yet." She bent down the best she could. undid the tube on the tire, and used a pen to make the air come out.

"You done?" We turned around and Kruz was standing there with the lawyer lady, who had her phone out.

"I am now." She stuck her finger up, sat in the front seat and told me to come on.

"Let her know that's no longer my truck because I'm waiting for my brand-new one. Jamaica is supposed to drop it off here."

"Huh? If it's not yours, why is it here?"

"I wanted to ride in it one last time. The tow truck is here to pick it up and look, there's Jamaica dropping my new one off." I saw Rhythm turn her head when the tow truck dude came and my fiancé. Jamaica handed him the keys to a brand-new Maserati truck. The shit was beautiful too.

"You buying new trucks nigga?" Rhythm started in the direction of the truck.

"If you even think about breathing on it, I'll snap your got damn neck in this parking lot." Rhythm stopped short and looked at him. Something about the way he said it, had us both shook and he ain't even talking to me.

"Get in the fucking car and go home."

"You don't tell me what the fuck to do." He smirked and walked over to her. I ran over to get in the middle.

"These tantrums don't do shit but make my dick hard." She sucked her teeth.

"When you finish acting like a six-year-old, bring your ass home." He kissed her cheek and walked off. I couldn't do shit but laugh.

"Y'all get on my nerves." I told her and pushed her towards the car.

"Take me home."

"Which house?" She snapped her neck at me.

"I'm just saying because he said.-"

"Fuck you Kalila. I ain't going nowhere near hm." She shouted and I laughed. These two are their own worst enemies.

****

"Those two are crazy." I told my mom after filling her in on what went down yesterday at the restaurant.

Rhythm calls herself not speaking to me today because I didn't agree with the way she handled shit. That, and the fact I pulled up in front of the house her and Kruz stayed at. I sat there for a good twenty minutes waiting for her to get over herself and get out. Unfortunately; she stayed put. I eventually had to drive her to Sayreville.

"They'll get it together."

"You think so?" I opened the door to the cake testing place. Jamaica and I set the date and, in a few months,, I'll be his wife.

"Yea because the drama only stems from your sister. Once she's outta the picture it'll be smooth sailing for everyone." I signed in and stared at my mom.

"What? I already told your sister the reverend is waiting on my call for the services." I felt bad because as a mother, no one ever wants to hurt a child. However; with a sister like Zahra who can blame her?

144

"Well it's her fault anyway." The lady came over and escorted us to the back. She had a weird look on her face. I paid it no mind until she returned with two cakes and insisted we try the chocolate one. My mom picked a spoon up and went to dip into it.

"Hold on." I stood and went to the back. Even with the lady yelling for me not to enter because it's not allowed, I kept going. There were two other women who themselves looked petrified. One gave me eye contact and gestured with her head for me to look out the window. I did and ran back to the front.

"Let's go." I snatched my mom up along with my things.

"Thanks for stopping by and I'm sorry you didn't like the cake." My mother looked at her crazy, where I knew the exact reason she did it. She wanted the people to think I had no idea they were in the back.

When the woman had me look outside, there were two big black trucks. I had no idea who the guys were but Kandy stood on the opposite side and her face is not one I'd ever forget. She had the nerve to be on the phone laughing like she wasn't tryna kill me.

Who makes plans to kill someone and instead of watching, finds time to bullshit around? You're supposed to get in, do the job and bounce. That right there let me know she's an amateur and it's no telling what else her ass had in store for me.

"I don't know where she came from and I'm so sorry." The woman whispered.

"Who is she talking about?"

"You need to get yourself and staff outta here."

"They have people watching. Please call the police." Her eyes were tearing up. I picked my phone up and called Jamaica.

"What's up sexy? The cake better be the bomb."

"Babe, she's here."

"Say no more." He hung up and I told the woman to have her staff try and remain calm. I don't know how she's gonna do it but at least I did my part.

"What's going on Kalila?" I stopped in front of my car and something told me not to get in. I didn't hit the alarm and flagged down a cab going by.

"Why are we in a cab?"

"Press this." I handed my mother the key fob as the driver pulled off.

BOOM! The ground shook and so did a few cars. I didn't bother turning around because my suspicions were correct. Not only did Kandy try and poison me in the cake store, she had someone put a bomb under my car.

"I'm fine." I answered because soon as the bomb went off, so did my phone.

"I'm gonna get her babe. I swear, I am."

"Hurry because this is started to be ridiculous. It never takes you this long to find someone." I only knew that because we always spoke about some of the killings he did. He said, they have a person in mind, find them and get it over with. For some reason it was taking a long time with her and my sister.

"Go home ma and I'll be there soon." We hung up and I rested my head on my mother's shoulder. I really hope he gets her because between her and Zahra, they doing too much.

I hated to hear my girl being upset but I had no idea the bitch Kandy would know where she'd be. Unfortunately; she found her at a damn cake shop. It made me wonder if she's aware of all the places Kalila had set up to go. I have to make her change up and send security with her. I have someone following her at all times but it seems like I'm gonna need to send them inside the places with her.

My girl is definitely a fighter but when it comes to that street life; she ain't with it. It's been plenty of times that she had a hard time dealing with death. Shit, she just stopped having nightmares about the guy she murked in the motel room. I ended up killing the dudes who were watching over that spot because they were sloppy as hell.

Ain't no way my girl and Rhythm, should've been able to make it past the doorway. It makes me think the guy who was there wanted them to come in. Especially, after we found out his background.

Now we conduct business at the warehouse and only use that one for emergencies. I think its more piece of mind for

Kruz and I. Well more him now because Kalila has a different job. Kruz has been tryna get his wife to stop working there but she stubborn just like him. They say opposites attract but what is it called when you're more alike than anything?

"Is everyone here?" I asked Drew who pulled up with a few other guys.

"Yea. Is this gonna be like the other spot?"

"I'm not sure because I've never really spoken with the brother." He nodded and all of us got in position.

KNOCK! KNOCK! I banged on the door and peeped our surroundings. We were in a suburban area that held mostly whites.

Each house was about half a mile or so from the next. We didn't wanna show up in packs and make someone contact the cops. Therefore; the rest of the crew was down the street.

"Who is it?" Kruz looked at me and I shrugged my shoulders.

"It's Peter. Can I borrow some brown sugar?" I shook my head at him using the line from Bad Boys. He's been tryna use it forever.

"Peter?" You heard the locks coming off and the door opened.

If I weren't with Kalila, I'd take this white chick upstairs. She was definitely pretty with a petite body. You could tell she worked out and her dark brown hair rested on her shoulders. Her lips may have Botox in them but they'd look good around my dick. I had to shake the thought because it's not what I'm here for.

"Can I help you?" She had an innocent look until she noticed Kruz and Drew.

"Where's Ricardo?"

"Why do you need him?"

"We need to ask him some questions about his sister." You heard her suck her teeth.

"Move bitch!" Kruz pushed past.

"Excuse me! You don't just walk in my house."

"Who is it babe?" We looked up and noticed Kandy's brother walking with a towel on. I cocked my gun and shot a hole right past his nose.

"What the hell?" He put his hands up and stared down at his wife.

"There looking for one of your sisters. I'd have to say Kandy because Margie is dead." She said it with no feeling whatsoever.

"Whatever she did, I'm not a part of."

"When's the last time you been to your fathers?"

"I haven't seen my father in three years." Kruz led him down the steps.

"Why is that?"

"I don't approve of the lifestyle he leads."

"I can't tell." I waved my hand around the mansion.

"This is my wife's money and I'm a lawyer, therefore I have my own."

"What do you want from him? Money? I'll give it to you if the two of you leave and never return."

"We don't want no money."

"Please don't kill us." His wife shouted. Kruz tossed him against the wall with his wife.

"I have a proposition for you since I can tell you're not lying."

"What is it?"

"In your father's home, Margie mentioned him having inside walls. Which house is it and how do I get in?"

"Oh, that's easy. My father has a place in Edison. No one really knows about it because he's barely there."

"How do you know then if you don't fuck with him?"

"He's had the house for years so when my stepmother pissed him off, that's where he'd stay. He always said if any of us needed to hide from enemies, we should go there."

"Word?" He nodded.

"There's an entire apartment down there. A kitchen, bathroom, living room and another door to lead outside."

"Sounds like a maze." Kruz said and looked at me.

"A maze we're about to have fun traveling through." Drew was souped. He loved doing crazy shit.

"How do we get in the crib? How many guards at this place and how do I get in the walls?"

"There used to be two guards there at all times and you get in by using a code." We looked at him.

"I'll give you mine as long as you don't kill me." Kruz glanced over at me.

"This is what's gonna happen." I stood in front of them.

"I'm gonna leave my boy Trevor and another guy here. When we get to the house if what you say is true, you have my word that I won't kill you. If it's a lie.-"

"IT'S NOT A LIE. I SWEAR." He shouted nervously.

"How do I get in the walls?"

"In the library, there's a big black book with no title. Push it forward once and pull it back. The wall will open and lead you down the stairs."

"Well damn. What kinda shit he on?"

"Exactly the reason I can't be around him."

"Because he has a secret part to his house?"

"No because his lifestyle has torn this family apart. My sister Margie is dead, you're about to kill Kandy and they just found my mother's body a couple of days ago. I don't want anyone else to die, so if you find my father there, do me a favor

154

and kill him too. At least, me and my family won't have to be paranoid anymore."

"Family?"

"Yes. We have three kids and they are at her parents for the night. Can you please do this and make the call for them to leave. I don't want my kids to come home and see strangers with guns on their parents. No offense." He looked at Trevor who waved him off.

"One last thing."

"Yea."

"Who's gonna take over when your father dies?" He ran his hand over his face.

"Unless he changed it; me." I looked at Kruz who shook his head. This nigga specifically told us we'd get it if he died.

"Honestly; I don't want it. If you kill him feel free to take everything. I'll sign it all over to you two except any life insurance policies he may have going to my kids."

"Bet."

"Can my wife grab me some clothes?"

155

"Y'all can do what you want in the house except make phone calls or get on the computer. Pretend as if Trevor and the other guy are visiting." I shrugged and walked out with Kruz.

"What you think?" We made our way to the car.

"I think we about to be the motherfucking connect nigga."

"Word!" We started laughing and pulled out to go get rid of Mr. Euburne and his daughter.

****

"Damn, he must have her here. Look at all these niggas posted up." Kruz and I looked around and there were men with guns all over. Lucky for us, we had shooters everywhere.

"You ready?" I asked Kandy's brother. At first, I wasn't gonna take him but after he mentioned all the security it would've been harder to even get on the premises quietly.

"I don't have a choice." He pressed his number on the gate and it opened slowly. We pulled in and each guard we passed went down, one by one. Due to the darkness, it was very easy.

When he pulled up to the front door, it opened and out stepped his pops. Now I had no real beef with this man because to my knowledge he was assisting in finding his daughter for me. Who knew he had been playing me the entire time? This motherfucker had me going on wild goose chases and then would say, *I just missed her*; knowing damn well she wasn't anywhere he said.

"Son! Are you going to get out?" He reached out with both arms wide, while dude stayed in the car.

You could tell he wasn't beat. Thank goodness the tint on the back window was dark enough he couldn't see through. We didn't need him aware of our presence because he could say one word and have the car riddled with bullets.

"What you want me to do?" He asked through gritted teeth so his father wouldn't know we were in the car.

"Get out, go inside and shut the door without locking it." He turned the car off and did as we said. I noticed three bodies fall off the roof at the same time the door closed. Again, timing was everything.

"Let's get this nigga so I can go home and get my dick sucked or wet."

"When Rhythm come back?"

"When the fuck we done here." I busted out laughing.

"What? A month is long enough for her petty ass tantrum."

"You do know it's your fault."

"Whatever." I shook my head and left him standing there.

"Yo, this shit is trash." I whispered when we opened the door. For him to be the connect, the house looked like shit. Trash everywhere, shitty ass furniture and anything else that goes in a nasty house. It smelled like somebody took a shit and the sewer is backed up too. I'm all for being incognito but this is ridiculous.

"Why haven't I seen you?" I guess he wasn't lying about them not speaking.

"Doesn't really matter because you won't be seeing him after this." Mr. Euburne was shocked as hell to see us but nothing prepared him for what's coming.

158

PHEW! I made a perfect shot in between his eyes. His body hit the ground hard as hell.

"I'm outta here." I yanked dude up by the shirt and made him point out the room. He walked with us, pointed to the book and started looking in the desk for whatever.

"Yo! This is nice." Drew had some glass vase looking thing in his hand.

I shook my head, drew my gun and walked down the steps with my brother and boy behind me. The stairs were spiral and at first you only saw walls. When we reached the bottom it definitely resembled an apartment like the son said. The television was on in the living room and something was cooking on low in the kitchen. It made this much easier because when we set this shit on fire, we can say the stove was left on.

I opened the door to the bedroom and wasn't surprised at all. Kandy was riding the guy, who I'm assuming is Geoffrey.

"You should be more careful about who you let come in." Kandy jumped off and the dude tried to reach for something. Kruz shot his hand off.

"FUCK!"

"What do you want Jamaica?"

"Why couldn't you just move on?" She covered her body with a sheet. It didn't matter because I drug her off the bed by her hair.

"She doesn't deserve you Jamaica."

"Why is that?"

"Because you were promised to me and we made a pact. You were doing your own thing as it was, so why even get a divorce?" She had the nerve to be crying. Meanwhile, her man is damn near dying from his hand being shot off and the blood pouring out.

"You sound stupid."

"Why because I still love you? Or because I would've done anything to make you love me the way I loved you."

"All this shit you talking is corny."

"Corny huh? Was it corny when we almost killed you in the hospital?"

"That was you?"

"Yup and if the dumb bitch he used to go with didn't shoot first, we would've had you." With her running her mouth, all she did is prove her death is a must.

"Why you going after my wife though? She ain't did shit to you."

"Your wife? You married her already?"

"Our business doesn't concern you. Why did you go after her?"

"I told you, she doesn't deserve you. You and I were supposed to run the empire after my father."

"Kandy, you got a whole nigga with you. And what happened to your baby?" Not that I cared but for someone who tried to get me to stay with her, she was allegedly pregnant.

"There wasn't a baby."

"WHAT?" The dude yelled as much as he could.

"Jamaica, let's just go. It can still be about us."

"Its over Kandy." I placed my gun on her forehead and pulled the trigger. The gun went through her skull and her head exploded.

"Your turn." I stared at the dude.

"Wait!"

"There is no wait. You sent those niggas to rob us and tried to kill us in the hospital. You ran outta lives my nigga." I wasted no time getting rid of him.

"I'm happy as hell this shit is over." I put my gun in my waist and the three of us checked everything in the house. Anything we thought may have info on it, we took and destroyed the rest in a small fire set on the stove.

We made the fire look like a grease one because it would burn faster. Who cares if the coroner found out they were murdered first? All I know is my fiancé can sleep better and go places without being watched.

"Let's go." I snatched Rhythm up by the ankles, put those ugly ass Ugg slippers on her feet and stood her up.

"What the hell are you doing?" She wiped the eye boogers out and tried to focus.

It was after three in the morning and we had just finished getting rid of Mr. Euburne, Kandy and the Geoffrey nigga. I was horny as hell and ready to go home and fuck. A month is a long time with no pussy for a nigga like me. Granted, I could've had my share of women but still being married; I respected my vows. I'll never have my wife looking like a fool in these streets.

Rhythm on the other hand was doing whatever she wanted. I know she was mad at what I said, and I get it but one... you don't put your hands on me and two... we married. You don't get mad at something I say and throw what we had away. What she think this is?

"You need any of this shit before we go?"

"Kruz, I'm not leaving. It's three in the morning and we're getting divorced remember?" She crawled back on the bed and I smacked the hell outta her ass.

"Owww!"

"I'm not gonna tell you again to come on." She rolled her eyes and placed her arms on top of her big ass stomach.

"Ok fine." I turned to walk out and smirked. She wanna play games I got something for her ass.

"THAT'S RIGHT! AND DON'T BRING YOUR ASS BACK. She barked and I kept walking. I went to my truck, grabbed the small cage and stepped back in the house. I opened the room door and she had the nerve to be under the covers tryna go back to sleep. It's all good.

"You not coming right?"

"No Kruz. Now go." She kept the covers over her face which made this much easier.

"A'ight. I'm out." I lifted the cage, peeled the cover a little, let my little friends out, went downstairs and sat on the couch. I turned the TV on, put my feet on the table and waited.

"Three, two, one." My phone rang. I picked it up and didn't even say hello.

"OH MY GOD!!!! KRUZ COME BACK HERE! PLEASEEEEEEEEEE! OH MY GOD!!!!"

"What Rhythm?"

"Kruz, please come back. There are two snakes in the bed, well they're on the floor because I kicked them off. Please come get me."

"Why would I do that? You told me to leave and you don't wanna be bothered."

"Kruz, I'm sorry. Please help me. Oh my God they're tryna get back on the bed. KRUZZZZZ! Please." I could hear her starting to cry.

"You lucky I'm still here. I'll be right up." I shut the TV off and took my time going up the stairs.

"I don't see any snakes Rhythm." She had her back against the headboard, standing on her feet in a squatting position. She had tears running down her face and literally using the remote to try and hit them if they got close to the bed. I ain't even gonna lie; I was cracking the fuck up.

165

"Right there Kruz. Look." She pointed to the floor. I bent down and picked one up.

"Rhythm these snakes little as hell." I brought it closer to her and she damn near had a heart attack.

"STOPPPPPPP!" Her head was pressed against the wall and she was terrified to look. I swear I almost cried from laughing so hard.

"Let me put them back in the cage before Drew gets mad." He loved snakes and had a few pythons and Boa's at his house. I damn sure wasn't bringing those so I settled for these garter snakes.

I picked the other one up and went downstairs to get the cage. I heard stomping across the floor and then down the steps. I turned and folded my arms across my chest.

"Kruz." She had her two index fingers rubbing her temples.

"I know you didn't bring those snakes here and put them under the covers."

"Actually, I did."

"You play too much." She pushed me in the chest almost making me fall over the coffee table behind me.

"Still got a hand problem."

"Whatever." She went to walk away and I grabbed her hand.

"Let's go."

"I'm not.-" I grabbed her by the back of the night shirt, picked up the keys, snakes and walked out the front door.

"I'm gonna fall." She was tripping over her own feet.

"Are you gonna walk to my truck?"

"No."

"Then you'll be getting there like this because you way too big for me to carry you."

"Lord, why did you place this man in my life?"

"Too late to ask him questions now. You should've done that before you sampled this good ass dick. Now get in." I opened the passenger side door and she refused until I gave her a look to let her know I'm done playing.

"Why are you here? Aren't you supposed to be dividing up our assets?" She asked when I got in the driver's seat.

"Rhythm ain't nobody getting a divorce so calm the fuck down."

"Ugh ahh. I do not appreciate how you're talking to me."

"Then pipe the hell down." I pulled off and started driving home.

"This temper tantrum is over and if you wanna sleep in another room; fine."

"I don't wanna be around you." She kept staring out the window.

"Too got damn bad. We married Rhythm and there are no breaks." I was getting frustrated with this baby acting shit.

"Kruz."

"I'm serious. I should've never asked you about Zahra being at the motel and if you knew. You had no business smacking me or tearing up my old truck." She sucked her teeth.

"All that shit is over and it's time to move on."

"What if I don't want to with you?"

"Too bad. It's til death do us part and I'ma damn sure be the only one you deal with until you die." She snapped her neck.

"Now after I fuck some sense in your ass, feel free to sleep in any room you want except the master bedroom."

"Wait a minute?"

"What? You wanna suck me off instead? I'm down for whatever because a nigga to release bad."

"Ain't nobody fucking you and why can't I sleep in the master bedroom? I picked that furniture out." She had the nerve to pout.

"My wife picked that furniture out and since you're acting like a chicken head, you can sleep in a hotel bed like they would." I shrugged my shoulders. Those mattresses in the guest rooms were horrible.

"I can't stand you."

"Whatever." I parked in the driveway after the gate closed.

"Back to what I was saying. We fucking or you sucking?" She hopped out the truck and slammed the door.

169

"You mess this truck up and I promise to fuck you until your water breaks."

"Please open the door. I can't listen to anymore of your shenanigans."

"I'll open it when I feel like it." I leaned on the wall with my leg up and stared in the sky.

"You ever wonder..."

"KRUZZZZZZ OPEN THE DOOR!"

"A'ight yo. Why you yelling?" I put the key in the door and watched her push it open. She turned around and stared at me.

"I know damn well you weren't expecting a welcome home party." Jamaica told me about the surprise he gave Kalila that night at his condo. Ain't no way in hell Rhythm getting any shit like that from me with the way she's acting. Always talking about chicks need to grow up and stop throwing tantrums and she be the main one.

"AHHHHHH!" She stormed up the steps, went in one of the rooms and closed the door. Rhythm can be mad all she wants but she'll be mad in this house and that room. Tha fuck she think this is?

****

BANG! BANG! BANG! BANG! I ignored the door and continued watching television.

BANG! BANG! BANG! BANG! I blew my breath out and walked slowly to the door.

"What?" Rhythm pushed past me and to the bed.

"Do you really need the volume that loud?"

"I can't get the full affect if it's low." She stood with the remote pointed at the TV and turned it down.

"Well her pussy dry and his dick look like it hurts going in and out." She referenced the porn video I was currently watching. It's been a few days since she's been back and as much as I wanted her, I was still combing the streets day and night tryna find Zahra. No one had seen her and I made sure to have someone watching her mother's because all bitches go home.

"How you know it's dry?"

"Your dick not even hard watching it." She pointed to my dick in my basketball shorts.

"Not the point. How you know she dry?"

"Ugh, I watched this one before and..."

"You watched it and you talking shit to me?"

"Because it don't have to be loud. If you really wanna get your dick hard, you should watch this one." She went to the closet and pulled out the box we kept pornos in.

"What's this?" I ran in the closet and it was too late. Rhythm's entire face dropped along with her mouth as the walls went in and my toys came into view.

"Unmmm, this is a lot." Her head went around the closet.

"This is nice." She picked up the brand-new hunters knife I purchased. It was made outta titanium with a snake like handle.

"You always in my shit." I popped her hand and took it from her.

"This our shit remember?"

"Oh, we married again?" I pressed the button and the walls disappeared.

"How did you find this?" I pointed to the button to display my toys. It was camouflaged with the wall and you'd only know it was there if I told you.

"It's where I put the box of videos. My arm must've brushed against it by accident because I damn sure had no idea it existed."

"Don't let me catch yo ass in here."

"Maybe. Maybe not but I know where my weapon is to kill you." I ignored her because we both know she ain't crazy.

"Anyway. I'm going to shower." She put a DVD in and walked out. I couldn't do shit but smile. My wife can play all the games she wants but she knows where home is.

I turned the shower on, waited for it to get hot and stepped in. The water felt amazing hitting my skin but then again, my fingers were circling my clit. I lifted my leg high as possible, leaned back on the shower wall and reminisced on the last time Kruz had my pussy in his mouth. I loved the way he took his time to please me and every part of my body. Sex with him is never boring and I cum so much it puts me straight to sleep.

"You knew exactly what you were doing turning that video on." I heard Kruz and refused to stop because the orgasm was right there and I needed it.

"I do miss watching you."

"Mmmmmph." He inserted two fingers inside as I continued playing with myself. Not even a minute later did I explode.

"Fuck! I needed that." I tried to control my breathing but it was no use because he swung me around, put both of my hands over my head on the wall with his on top, and rammed himself inside. My body shook vigorously and each time he pumped, I cried out in ecstasy.

"You still my wife Rhythm?" He now had a fistful of my hair in his hands, with my face turned to his. One leg was in the crook of his other arm and yet my arms were still above my head on the wall.

"I can't hear you."

"Ahhhhh!" He dug deeper. My face contorted into something crazy and he had the nerve to smirk.

"Yesssssss. Kruz yes I'm your wife." He let my leg down, turned me around and put both hands on side of my face.

"I play a lot Rhythm, but when I say; til death do us part, I mean it. Ain't no other nigga gonna ever say he had you." He forced his tongue in my mouth and took control. I had my arms around his neck and let the tears flow. I loved him with all that I had and to know he still loved me the same, made me cry. I really didn't think we were gonna make it.

The whole time we didn't speak, he never called, refused to stop by and didn't call me to see Axel. I know it was me who said we should get a divorce but I was mad and threw a damn tantrum. I blame him because he spoiled me with his love and affection and when it was gone, I didn't know how to act.

"Stop crying." I nodded my head as he wiped the tears.

"Shit, I'm about to cum Rhythm." I squeezed my muscles together and felt him fill me up. His breathing was fast at first and then slowed down. My back was to his chest and I could feel his heart beating when I laid my head on it.

"I'm not finished with you." He trailed kisses down my neck and rubbed my stomach.

"We got a month to make up for."

"Oh yea." I turned with a smile on my face and got as low as I could to give him what he wanted. We stayed in the bed the entire day making up and I must say it was worth it.

****

"How can I help you?" I asked Teddy who was behind the window at the motel. Today was my last day here and instead of calling out, I came in. Looking at him, I probably should've stayed home.

"You really having a baby by that nigga?" I placed my phone down after texting Kruz he was here and tried my best to stay calm. He's the aggressive type of nigga who don't know how to take a hint.

"How can I help you Teddy?" I asked again.

"Where's all my stuff from room 213?"

"213?"

"Yea bitch, 213."

"When did you have the room here?" I pulled the information up on the computer and his name wasn't there.

"Over a month ago."

"A month ago? Let me check." I did a little more research and the only time he could be mentioning is when Zahra was here.

"Hurry the fuck up." I rolled my eyes.

"Teddy, your name is not in the system and…"

"You dumb bitch I had it under my cousins name. You think I'm that stupid to put it under my own?"

"You can go Teddy."

"I ain't going nowhere until you get my shit. Now DO IT!" He made me jump when he shouted but I didn't back down.

"Get the fuck outta here before I call the cops."

"Call them. By the time, they get here, I'll have tasted that pussy Kruz bugging over and sliced your throat."

"Are you seriously talking about raping a pregnant woman?" I had my arms folded and looking at him with disgust.

"It won't be rape because Zahra said you love for me to get aggressive in the bedroom."

"Zahra?" I was shocked he mentioned her, then it clicked how they most likely stayed in the room together hiding out.

"Don't you worry though. I'll make sure your dead body gets delivered to Kruz."

"No need. Tell me where Zahra is and I'll go with you." He crossed me as a dummy and someone I could get over with.

"Yea right."

"I give you my word. If you give me her whereabouts I'll let you taste my pussy. Hell, why not let you fuck me? It will be a way to get back at Kruz for this bullshit he has me caught up in with his ex." I could see him struggling with it.

"All I have to do is tell you where she is?"

"That's it." I put my hand on the doorknob and smiled at the person standing outside that Teddy was unaware of.

"She's been with me at my sisters. Now open up so I can come in."

"You got it." I opened the door at the same time the office one opened.

"I hope she throws it on you the way she does me but then again, you ain't about to get shit."

BAM! Kruz pistol whipped him over and over. Blood was gushing out his head and eye. I had to scream for him to stop because he was in a zone.

"Zahra is at his sisters."

"How you know and get me some towels." I walked away and came back to see two big dudes taking Teddy out.

Kruz took the towels and wiped off his hands. He removed a lighter out his jeans and lit them on fire right outside the motel.

"I told you not to bring your ass in." He backed me in a corner.

"Am I in trouble daddy?" He smiled and as always melted my heart.

"Long as you know what's up later."

"Why did you come in? I thought the guy outside would."

"I told him to wait because I wanted Teddy. If he thought things were bad he had every intention of coming in."

"How can I ever repay you for saving me?"

"Delivering my baby so I can fuck you hard like I used to."

"What?" I put my hands on my hips.

"You be complaining in certain positions. I wanna be able to toss your little ass around like before."

"You're an ass."

"That's what they say." He grabbed my hand and asked if I had all my things because the replacement was walking in.

"Yup. I'm finally done with this place." I turned and took one last look at the job that kept my head above water.

"I'm gonna miss it."

"Stop being dramatic." He shook his head and helped me in his truck.

"Where to?" He asked and I told him to eat. I was hungry as hell.

WHAP! I punched Teddy in the face again for the hundredth time. I was at the warehouse beating his ass for not only tryna come for Rhythm, but for keeping Zahra protected knowing I had a hit out on her ass. He can't say he was in love with her because he didn't know her like that or maybe he did. Whatever the case, he should've turned her over.

"Why were you helping Zahra?" He could barely keep his head up and blood was dripping from damn near every part of his body.

"You killed my family." I heard him whisper and made him say it again.

"Let me get this right." I removed the plastic gloves off my hand, threw them away, pulled a chair up and sat in front of him.

"You were fucking Zahra because I killed your family?" He barely shook his head yes.

"So, we're just gonna skip over the fact you stole from us. It may not have been a lot but you still took it."

"You didn't have to kill all of them."

182

"Bro, you've been around long enough to know how this goes." I stood and pulled my gun out.

"You so busy tryna get me back for killing your family, that you just got your sister killed too."

"Huh?"

"She let y'all stay there right?" He remained quiet.

"No need to keep secrets now. Bring her in." Jamaica drug his sister in and tossed her on the ground next to him.

"Please don't kill me. I don't know what he did but I have no parts in it."

"Did you let Zahra stay at your house?"

"Who?"

"The bitch he fucking."

"Teddy didn't bring a chick to my house and if he did I've never seen her because he knows I didn't want anyone there." You could tell by the tone in her voice it's a possibility she didn't know.

"Oh well. You know now and the fact you're here means you wanna die."

"I didn't bring myself here."

183

"Not technically but your brother brought you here when he used your crib to stash the bitch. Don't worry though. You two are about to see each other again in hell and you can kill each other."

"Bro, they'll be dead already."

"Exactly! Which means they won't die again." I busted out laughing. I know some of the shit I said didn't make sense but it's still funny.

"Please don't." She cried out.

"Thank your brother."

Phew! Phew! I shot both of them in between the eyes, grabbed my keys and headed to Teddy's sister house to get the one person I've been waiting for.

I know people wanna know why Zahra didn't die in the beginning, but let me be the first to say, all good things come to those who wait. She ain't good but you know what I'm saying. Oh, and the fact I didn't know where she was didn't help. But it's in the past now so it's time to take her out her misery.

****

"Dang bro. These are nice!" Kash eyes were big as hell looking at the new Lebron's and Jordan's he got for his birthday. Kommon didn't know what to get him and since I already purchased the new 4K PlayStation he wanted, I told him Kash wanted those too.

My mother decided to throw him a party at their house. My dad was against it because he said Kash got into too much trouble and didn't deserve it. Somehow, she convinced him to have it and I don't wanna know how. I do see how much better they're getting along now that Zahra has nothing to hold over her head.

"I'm glad you like them."

"What did your sexy girlfriend get me?" Sabrina rolled her eyes.

"Yo! What I tell you about that shit?"

"I'm just saying bro. How you gonna bring a sexy woman home and think I'm not supposed to say anything?"

"Nigga you 10."

"Correction. I'm 11 now and just so you know my girl is gonna be bad too."

"Boy hush up and finish opening your gifts." My mom popped him on the head and told him to stop being rude and disrespectful.

"Fine. Kruz what did your fine wife get me?" I didn't even bother to entertain his shit.

"Here Kash." She handed him a small box and Axel was more excited for him to open it then anyone.

"What is it bro?" He's been calling Axel is brother for a while now and Axel been eating it up.

"It's a few games and money."

"AXEL!" We all yelled and he shrugged his shoulders.

"That's why you're the best brother ever." He gave him a hug and opened the gift grinning. The other kids looked on with amazement as he continued opening his presents. By the time he finished this punk had a lot of shit.

The DJ started playing some song that had all those fast ass girls tryna twerk. When Kalila, Sabrina and even my pregnant ass wife got out there it was like a damn battle. The little girls were trying but our women had them beat, hands down.

After the party was over, all of us were sitting on the front porch chilling and having our own time. My mom glanced over at me and I nodded by head. She came over to where Rhythm and I sat and asked to speak with her in private. She's been tryna get in my wife's good graces for a while now but Rhythm is stubborn as hell. However; I don't blame her because my mother did try and come for her at the restaurant when they first met.

"Babe, what does she want? I don't have time to be going into early labor for swinging off."

"Stop being so damn violent."

"Violent? You got some nerve after all the things you do."

"It's for the good of this family."

"Yea whatever." I smacked her on the ass and shook my head at her grabbing Kalila and Sabrina to go with her.

"It's time son." My father said and all of us went inside without saying a word. I locked the doors, made sure the kids were sleep and waited for my wife to finish.

187

When Kruz's mother called me in the house to talk, I didn't wanna go. Yes, we say hello and goodbye but that's it. I really don't have much to say because of the shit with Zahra. I could care less about her liking me. It's about Sasha missing out on time with her father and the fact she went so hard for a woman Kruz no longer wanted.

I grabbed Kalila and Sabrina with me because if I needed to smack her, they'd step in. Plus, if I laid hands on her at eight months pregnant, it's a guarantee my husband would kill me. Never mind I'd go into labor and if I lost my baby I wouldn't be the same. To avoid all of it, my girls being by my side is the best option.

She stopped in front of a small shed in the backyard, pulled a key out and unlocked the humongous lock on it. All three of us looked at her crazy because we wanted to know what was inside. We tried to move past her but she put her hand out and asked me if she could speak first.

"Rhythm, I want to apologize to you from the bottom of my heart. It was never my intention to be the type of mother

188

who dislikes a woman one of my sons chooses." I folded my arms.

"I admit Zahra has been around for a few years and yes I wanted my son to be with her." I sucked my teeth and so did Kalila and Sabrina. Don't nobody wanna hear that shit.

"You see, I'm old school and my kids were brought up with both biological parents in the home. It's the same lifestyle I thought my grandkids should be brought up in as well. However; not only did Kruz, my husband and other son Kommon let me know it may not be possible; you did as well."

"Mmmm hmmm." Kalila mumbled.

"It took me some time to get out of my own way and part of it had to do with things in my past I didn't want revealed. Rhythm." She moved closer to me.

"I know it's gonna take time to forgive me but I'm also hoping that what I have in the shed will help you do it faster. I don't wanna miss my grand baby growing up."

"Ummmm." I didn't really know what to say.

"Don't think about anything right now except what's behind these doors."

"What's behind them?" She smirked and winked her eye. I turned to see my husband standing there drinking a beer and leaning on the doorframe of the house. His mom opened the shed and all of us were shocked.

"What the...? How in the hell did you...?"

Zahra was in a chair tied up with duct tape around her mouth. Her hair had blood in it and you could tell she hasn't eaten in days or at least it looked like she hadn't.

"Your husband made this possible." I turned again and all the guys were now on the back porch.

"You see, Zahra may be the reason my first grandchild is here but she's also the reason my sons fought and stopped speaking to me. I lost a lot of sleep tryna figure out a way to get back in their good graces."

"But she was missing." I walked in the shed and punched Zahra so hard in the face, her chair tipped over.

"RHYTHM!" I heard Kruz yell from the porch.

"Ok! I won't hit her again. I had to get that out." Kalila moved me out the way, asked Mrs. Garcia to help her pick Zahra up and smiled. Sabrina stood by me because she too is

190

pregnant and Kommon already shouted for her not to do anything from the porch.

"Are you ok sis?" Kalila asked surprising all of us. She wiped some dirt off her face and the tears falling down. Zahra tried saying something but you couldn't hear.

"I can't understand you."

SWISH! Kalila ripped the duct tape off her mouth.

"Ahhhhhh." She screamed out and moved her mouth in different motions; I guess to get used to using it again.

"Kalila you can't let them kill me. Sasha is your niece. How would she feel knowing they took me away from her?" I wanted badly to intervene but Kruz walked in and pulled me away.

"I brought her here for you to see she was caught but this is Kalila's moment."

"Huh?" I turned to see Jamaica coming towards us with a big ass pot.

"You'll see. Back up." Kommon came in and moved Sabrina away.

"No one is gonna kill you Zahra. I won't let them."

191

"What?' I was mad as hell because the bitch definitely had to go. Kalila glanced at me and smiled.

"Thank you so much sis. Thank you. Can you untie me?"

"No one is gonna kill you Zahra because I am." Zahra froze.

"Wh…What…" Zahra started stuttering and I knew then she was terrified.

"All these years, I use to think the relationship between Rhythm and I is what bothered you the most but that's never been the case."

"You can bring it baby." She gestured for Jamaica to bring the pot over.

"The hatred in your heart stemmed from me ever being born." Zahra sucked her teeth.

"You were the only child for four years and the moment I was born, you began to turn into someone else as mommy says. You broke all my toys, beat me up all the time and would lie and say I fell."

"Sis, I'm sorry. I was young." Kalila chuckled.

"Now you're sorry but you weren't back then. You hated me so much, you burned me with scalding hot water at the age of seven." Zahra put her head down as Kalila lifted her shirt a little. The burn was so bad she still had a scar that led under her arm and to her hip. It doesn't look like a fire victim's body but it's there.

"You wanted to be the only child and I got in the way. Isn't that right?"

"Be careful Kalila." Jamaica handed her the pot.

"I want you to feel the exact pain I did. I mean you aren't seven but the pain will still hurt." Kalila lifted the pot and poured it all over her body.

"AHHHHHHHH!" You could see some of her skin falling off. I turned my head and buried it in Kruz's chest for the moment.

"Oh, I forgot to tell you. This is hot grease." Zahra was creaming so bad, Jamaica had to put the duct tape back on her mouth. The neighborhood is quiet and we didn't need any other spectators.

"I want you to know Zahra that even though I'm gonna be the one to take your life, I still love you because you're my sister, and my niece's mother. Unfortunately, you won't see her grow up, go to preschool, attend any parties, or get married." Kruz sucked his teeth and I started laughing.

"My real sister Rhythm, will be the best mother for her and you won't ever be spoken of moving forward."

"Kalila are you sure?" I asked when Jamaica handed her the gun because she was crying. I know this is hurting her because regardless of everything she's gone through, Zahra is still her sister.

"If it's not my mother who takes her life, it has to be me."

"I understand Kalila but you're shaking and…"

"That's why I love you Rhythm. You've always had my back and know me better than I know myself sometimes."

"You're my sister K. Maybe Jamaica should do it."

"I'm fine." She hugged me and wiped her eyes.

BOOM! BOOM! A gun went off and all of us froze.

194

"What the fuck?" All of us turned towards the door and I stared into the eyes of my son holding the smoking gun.

"AXEL!" Kruz ran over and took it from him.

"She won't bother you anymore mommy. TiTi, are you ok? Did she hurt you too?"

"How in the hell? Kruz, what just happened?"

"Don't be upset mommy. Daddy's been taking me in the backyard to shoot. He said, I had to protect you if he or daddy Kruz couldn't. Mommy, she said she would kill you."

"Axel, you're seven years old and…" I dropped to my knees and started crying hysterical. I didn't want my son growing up being a killer.

"Am I going to jail?"

"HELL NO!" Kruz shouted. He took us out the shed and in the house. I was disappointed in his father and couldn't wait to call hm.

"Where did you get a gun Axel? Kruz, this is not ok."

"Daddy told me to keep it in my bookbag at all times in case she found us and no one could save us. I'm sorry mommy.

I just wanted to make sure she couldn't hurt you and TiTi anymore." I didn't know what to say.

"Axel, I'm taking the gun away and if your father has a problem with it, tell him to call daddy Kruz."

"I don't need it anymore daddy Kruz. It was only for Zahra."

"Sis, he did it for you. I know you're upset and I would be too but he was scared she'd take you away." Kalila sat next to me rubbing my back.

"I know but…"

"It's over now. Look at the guys talking to him. Rhythm, they're gonna make sure he knows the seriousness of a gun." Kruz, Jamaica, Kommon and Mr. Garcia had him in the living room talking.

"I'm gonna curse his father out. He had no right to show him how to use a gun."

"You're right and I would do the same but look at it from big Axel's point of view."

"He's gonna be fine Rhythm. Kids are more resilient then we think." Mrs. Garcia said and passed me something to drink.

"He was protecting his mommy."

"He's only seven."

"A seven-year-old who is smart and knows a lot more than he let his mommy know." She smiled and went to the other room and grabbed Sasha from her husband.

"I'm proud of you Kalila."

"If my nephew didn't do it, I was. She had to go Rhythm." I nodded my head and stared at my son listening to the guys. They weren't being mean or yelling. I'm happy he wanted to protect me but I still think he's too young to learn how to use a gun.

"He's gonna be fine babe." Kruz said walking to the truck. I looked down at Axel next to me and he was engrossed in the Nintendo switch.

"I hope so."

"You know we got him."

"He should've told me." Kruz had Axel get in the truck and closed the door.

"You have every right to be upset and trust me when I say, I'm gonna stop by and speak to him but in his defense, he wanted to make sure his son knew how to keep you safe."

"I get it but…"

"Rhythm a lotta stuff has gone down and he was making sure his son didn't lose his mother." He wiped my eyes and pecked my lips.

"You think he needs to see someone?"

"No but I have a few connects and I'll call them in the morning."

"Kruz, what if they call the cops and tell what he did?"

"I don't fuck with those type of people. The person he speaks to won't reveal anything and Axel will never see inside a jail cell even if he grew up to be like his stepdad."

"He better not."

"I doubt he'd wanna be in the streets. The lil nigga can't stay off the game long enough." We both laughed because my son is addicted to those games.

"We're gonna be fine Rhythm." He grabbed my hand and kissed the top of it.

"I know and thanks for always being there even when I'm being a brat."

"Always and forever."

"Always and forever." I repeated him and put my head back as we drove home. I loved my family and I pray Axel ain't one of those kids in the future who becomes infatuated with killing because I don't think I could handle anything happening to him.

One year later...

Kalila and Jamaica were married a month after Zahra's death and her mom couldn't be happier. She had the funeral two days later and didn't invite anyone because the body never made it to the morgue, which means they didn't do an autopsy. It was fine because she would never be spoken of again anyway. Kalila had another son and told Jamaica they're gonna continue having kids until she gets her girl. Ms. Bell, found herself a new man and they've actually discussed marriage as well.

Sabrina and Kommon welcomed a baby girl. Unfortunately, Sabrina almost died in the delivery room because the baby was so big, she ruptured something internally. She claims the only way they'll have another kid is through a surrogate but Kommon talked her into having another one in a year and they'll definitely have a C-section.

Kash still has the biggest crush on her and even brought home a girl that resembled her, only younger. The only problem with that is she got caught stealing from their parents' house and Mrs. Garcia had a fit. Mr. Garcia had to tell her that's the only type of women he'll attract because he's a klepto himself.

Kruz and I welcomed our baby girl a week after Zahra's death. She was beautiful as ever and resembled Sasha in many ways. Kruz said it was meant to be since he already changed the mothers name on her birth certificate to mine.

As far as Axel goes, he hasn't even spoken of Zahra and is still very addicted to the video games. If you're wondering if Kruz and I are still petty, yes, he is. I can get real petty sometimes but he has me beat. For instance, I wouldn't give him any sex the other day because I was sore and he threatened to put some more snakes in the bed if I didn't. I swear he's the worst but I wouldn't dare trade him in for anyone else. I loved that man with all my heart and he feels the same.

The End

Thank you all for making this series and the others a success. You have no idea how much you constantly motivate me to continue writing. Love you all and get ready for the next series because its guaranteed to keep you on the edge of your seat.

CPSIA information can be obtained
at www.ICGtesting.com
Printed in the USA
LVHW021051110819
627236LV00012B/667